Also by Alan Gibbons

An Act of Love
Blood Pressure
Caught in the Crossfire
The Dark Beneath
The Defender
The Edge
Julie and Me and Michael Owen Makes Three
Raining Fire
You Took My Son (from April 2015)

THE LEGENDEER TRILOGY

Shadow of the Minotaur
Vampyr Legion
Warriors of the Raven

THE LOST SOULS

Rise of the Blood Moon
Setting of a Cruel Sun

HELL'S UNDERGROUND

1. Scared to Death
2. The Demon Assassin
3. Renegade
4. Witch Breed

HATE

ALAN GIBBONS

Indigo

First published in Great Britain in 2014
by Indigo
This paperback edition first published
in Great Britain in 2015
by Indigo
an imprint of Hachette Children's Group
and published by Hodder and Stoughton Limited

Orion House
5 Upper St Martin's Lane
London WC2H 9EA
An Hachette UK Company

1 3 5 7 9 10 8 6 4 2

A catalogue record for this book is available
from the British Library

ISBN 978 1 78062 178 4

Printed in Great Britain by Clays Ltd, St Ives plc

www.orionbooks.co.uk

To the Lancaster family

AUTHOR'S NOTE

This novel is a work of fiction. The attack on Rosie is based on a real attack, but otherwise the characters spring from my imagination. Their words and actions are mine. Their life stories are mine. Hate crime, sadly, is all too real. It hurts. It kills.

I came to write my story after meeting Sylvia Lancaster at a teachers' conference a few years ago. Sylvia spoke before me. I didn't know what was coming. I listened with an increasing sense of horror as she told the audience how her daughter, Sophie, had died on 24 August 2007 after a savage attack on Sophie and her partner Rob in Stubbylee Park, Bacup, Lancashire.

It was an unprovoked assault. Rob and Sophie dressed alternatively. The attackers called them 'moshers' and 'freaks'. The young couple didn't die because of something they had done or said. They died because of the way they dressed. Hate crime comes in many forms: racism, sexism, prejudice against the disabled and the form it takes in this book, homophobia.

That night I went home to my own wife and kids. Rarely have I appreciated the preciousness of human life and the ease with which it can be snuffed out.

Simon Armitage wrote a marvellous play called *Black*

Roses. The play employs Sylvia's own words and the words Simon imagines Sophie's ghost would have used to stunning effect. I didn't want my novel to tread the same ground so I invented the character of Anthony and from there reimagined the aftermath of the attack Sophie suffered through the eyes of a number of invented characters. *Hate* is the result. I hope it does Sophie justice and honours all victims of bigotry and prejudice.

Alan Gibbons
Liverpool
October 2013

'You are not here! The quaint witch Memory sees
In vacant chairs, your absent images,
And points where once you sat, and now should be
But are not.'

Percy Bysshe Shelley

TEENAGE KICKS

Saturday, 10 August 2013

The last time I saw Rosie, she was getting on the bus with Paul. It was August and the air was thick with dust and petrol fumes on the Manchester road. Off to our left, on the far side of the housing estate, sun and shadow were playing tag on the hills. Some of the people at the stop noticed the young couple next to them. Rosie and Paul didn't seem to notice. They were used to the attention. I found myself smiling. Rosie never minded. Jewels glitter. It is in their nature. That's what they do. They shine while other people, like me, live their lives unseen.

Then Rosie did something out of character. She called to me across the road as I walked away. She was beautiful, so tiny and perfect, but she made her statement by the way she dressed. She was quiet; happy in the skin she had made for herself. So when she called my name it was unexpected.

'Eve,' she cried. '*Teenage Kicks*.'

Mum had been playing it just before we left. She had looked up from her assignment. She used YouTube as a distraction when she needed a break. It was the way our family was, I suppose. We communicated through music, recommended the songs we listened to and enjoyed together.

'Do you want to hear perfection?'

I remember Rosie wrinkling her nose, teasing. She loved it really. She adored music, any kind of music, not just the doomy stuff I heard coming through the wall, but Sugababes, Abba, anything at all. The Undertones played to the end, then I said I would walk with her to the stop. Paul strode along beside us while we talked.

'Eve. *Teenage Kicks*.'

And she started to dance, her long, black skirt swaying, her slender arms and small hands weaving patterns. It was as if she was drawing a portrait of her soul in the air. I danced too, copying her every move. The memory of the music played in my head and we laughed with each new twist and turn. Her hair swung and the hot sun was bright on her face. That's how I remember her, laughing and glowing in the bright play of the light. Then Paul tapped her on the shoulder and the bus came between us. I watched them settling into their seats and waved. One last time Rosie's arms fluttered. One last time I copied her. Then she was gone.

Gone forever.

Monday, 24 February 2014

I had that image of Rosie in my head when Jess's elbow jabbed my ribs, calling me back to Monday registration, the scraped chairs, the fitful yawns, the general air of boredom. In the corridor, a door slammed.

'Hey, look what the wind blew in.'

The newcomer had collar-length blond hair and fine features. He was tall, lean and athletic-looking, but there was an awkwardness about him that diminished him somehow, and made him seem smaller than he was. I watched him with growing curiosity. He was backing against the wall, as if trying to melt into it. I recognised something of myself in the guarded way he sidled into the classroom. Some people announce themselves to the world. Others dip beneath its scrutiny. I waited for Mrs Rawmarsh to introduce him. When she said his name my heart slammed.

'This is Anthony Broad.'

She pronounced it Anthony with the accent on the 'th' as in thump. I glimpsed Jess's lips repeating the three syllables silently. She could be so predictable. She's great, but the moment she falls for some boy it's as if she becomes him, adopting his rhythms of speech, his attitudes, his ideas, no matter how stupid they sound. Only when the first rush of attraction is over does she become herself again. I love her for her loyalty and fun, but sometimes the wild enthusiasms drive me crazy.

'You don't fancy him?'

We'd been here a few times now. Jess likes boys and they like her. She gets their attention with the way she walks, the way she talks, the intent way she listens, the infectious way she laughs. She makes everyone in her company feel special.

'What's not to fancy? He's fit. Oh, come on, Eve, lighten up.'

I had a different reason to dwell on his name. It walked into my mind and stood in a darkened corner like an uninvited guest at a wedding. That name . . . Broad. Anthony Broad.

Registration over, we shouldered our bags and stepped into the corridor. I felt the press of Jess's fingers on my forearm.

'Eve, pretend to say something to me. He's coming over.'

Why all the excitement? I refused to play Jess's games and stayed completely silent.

'Hi, Anthony.'

She was like one of those little terriers that rolls on its back and invites you to tickle its tummy. She was happy and bright-eyed, sending out signals without an iota of self-consciousness. What if it really was him? I rummaged in my bag for some imaginary object so I didn't have to make eye contact. I left that to Jess. She had all the eye contact of a peacock's tail. She was so, so eager to impress, and I was drowning.

Broad.

Anthony Broad.

'Do you think you could help me?' he mumbled. 'Everything is kind of confusing. How do I get to L29?'

'L is for Languages,' Jess explained. 'All the Arts and Humanities are down there. It goes English, Geography, History, Languages. It's alphabetical. Pastoral Care and RE are off to the right. Maths and Science are down the other end of the school. Zoology's at the end.'

'There's a Zoology department?'

'No. That was a joke.'

'Oh.'

Jess looked perturbed.

'Obviously not a very good joke,' she said.

Her wide eyes and pouting lips didn't seem to be working their usual magic. Anthony's mind was elsewhere. He didn't seem to have listened to a word she'd said.

'Oh, right.'

The second word dropped away, apologetic. His uncertain gaze followed the way she was pointing.

'I see.'

Jess giggled. She was dog whistle high and invitingly cute. Some boys like that. This best friend didn't.

'You don't get it at all, do you?'

I glanced his way and saw his uncertainty evolve into a thin smile.

'Not really.'

The crowds hurrying between classes buffeted us. Girls dissolved into laughter, boys leapt on their mates' backs, teachers weaved wearily through the tumult, casting the odd disapproving eye. Everybody had a purpose but, at the centre of the crush, Anthony didn't. For that moment he was the eye of the storm.

'Come with us. We're going to L29 too. Spanish, yeah?'

'Right. Spanish.'

I was willing Jess to stop. Why did she have to adopt him as if he was a stray dog? Surely he could find L29 by himself? Kids start new schools all the time. Why did she have to roll out the red carpet for this one? He could see where we were going. All he had to do was follow us. But Jess just chattered away.

'How come you moved school? People usually stay put in Year 11 – GCSEs and all that.'

Anthony looked uncomfortable. I could see the thoughts turning over in his mind. His face betrayed him as he considered first one answer then another. Jess came at it another way.

'Where was your last school?'

'Brierley.'

I heard the way he said it, as a kind of confession. Brierley. That's where it happened. In Cartmel Park. Oh God, my first instincts were right.

'Why did you move?'

There was that same moment of discomfort.

'Family stuff. You know.'

We reached L29. Anthony made a beeline for the back row and sat in the corner, by the window, staring out across the moors. I knew that distant look. I knew that aching detachment. But he was no kindred spirit. He was my opposite. Anthony Broad. It was him. It had to be. Jess frowned a question. What was I thinking? I smiled and shrugged. That seemed to reassure her.

Miss Munoz swept into the room, stopped, briefly registering Anthony's presence, then fumbled for the small grey remote to start the whiteboard projector.

It purred into life. The failing bulb cast a gloomy light on the screen. Dust motes swirled. Miss Munoz started the lesson the way she always did, with the date and the weather. Then she asked us all what we did over the weekend. Some made an effort. Some grunted. Others grinned and said something stupid to wind her up. Most of us just fidgeted and hoped she would pass us by.

It was Monday, 24 February, less than six months after that night, after what happened to Rosie.

At first, it looked like we were sharing all our classes with Anthony. He was there in Spanish, English and History. He wasn't there for Maths. Jess was disappointed. We were on our way out of the gates when she turned to me.

'You're very quiet.'

'I'm always quiet.'

'Yes, but not like this. You've hardly said a word all day. Are you sure you're OK? Have I done something wrong?'

I shook my head.

'Course not.'

'You sure?'

'Jess, it's not you. Forget it, OK?'

Jess was still working out how to probe further when something distracted her. Anthony was standing at the bus stop. He took time to register our presence.

'This is a coincidence,' Jess said, placing herself next to him. 'Fancy you getting the 25, same as us. Where do you live?'

Anthony described the parade of shops less than a mile from my house. There was a newsagent, a Chinese chippy, an Indian takeaway, a charity shop and two empty ones covered with posters. Jess went into gush mode.

'How amazing! We basically live either side of you. That's like, well, coincidence of the century.'

Hardly. Our little town of Shackleton wasn't New York or Nairobi.

'Did you hear that, Eve?'

I heard it. At the mention of my name Anthony turned. I looked away immediately, my cheeks burning. What was so amazing? He had to live somewhere. I only wished it wasn't close to me. The streets rushed by. Anthony crouched so he could recognise the parade, a sure sign he was new to the area.

'This is my stop,' he said and shoved his way to the doors.

I watched him go. Something in the way he held himself told me he knew. It was obvious that he had his ghosts, just as I had mine.

The door to the flat opened. The cramped rooms creaked a reluctant welcome. The walls were bare. There were no covers on the cushions, no photos on the mantelpiece. It was a work in progress. A carrier bag gaped open in a corner. There was a sheet of bubble wrap, some brown parcel tape, a torn label, the sure signs of a recent move. Anthony closed the door.

'Is that you, Anthony?'

This time it was Anthony with a 't', not a 'th'.

'Of course it's me. Who else were you expecting, Superman?'

'No need to be sarky.'

His mum made her way in from the kitchen. Gemma Broad was in her early forties, but she looked five years younger. She was slim and attractive but, like her son, she had a guardedness that dulled the glow of life.

'How was school?'

Anthony tried to disguise his momentary hesitation. He heard the catch in his mum's voice as she slapped the cloth on the coffee table.

'Been cleaning up?' he said hurriedly, hoping to gloss over his delay answering.

She ignored his attempt at diversion.

'Nice try, Anthony,' she said. 'Something's wrong. It's there in your voice. Let's hear it.'

It took a few moments for him to answer.

'There's this girl at school. I think she knows who I am.'

Something akin to panic washed over his mum's features.

'How? How is that possible?'

He was aware of the lorries rumbling down the road under the window, the roar of tyres. The panes shuddered slightly.

'Anthony?'

'She kept staring at me.'

His mum relaxed a little, recovering her composure.

'People stare for all kinds of reasons. It doesn't mean she knows.'

Anthony refused to be shifted from his conviction.

'She does. I'm sure of it. You should have seen the way she looked at me.'

'Anthony, you're making a mountain out of a molehill. You're paranoid.'

She left him alone with his thoughts. He could hear her in the kitchen, rinsing out the cloth, washing her hands, making a start on his tea.

'Sausage and beans?'

His reply was unenthusiastic. It had nothing to do with the food. He was still thinking about his first day at Shackleton Brow High School. He had been hoping for a new start. Was that too much to ask?

Leaning back on the sofa, he let his eyes close. He was back in Cartmel Park amid the brooding trees. Several pairs of scuffed trainers crunched on the winding paths. There was a spray-canned stone arch, a fenced-off boating lake where they used to have pedalos and rowing boats, a boarded-up café and, somewhere, in the hot, scented, summer's night a couple was approaching, a tall, rangy twenty-two-year-old man and his girlfriend two years younger. She was beautiful and quiet.

She was the girl who died.

Oli was already in when Jess walked through the door. He always beat her home these days. He loved his scooter. It was only 100cc, but it gave him the freedom he craved. His parents wondered whether they had done the right thing buying it for him. Oli didn't only use it to commute to school. He would zip off in the evenings for hours on end without giving any clue where he was going.

'You the only one in?'

Oli dangled a leg over the arm of the chair and yawned.

'Dad won't be in until after seven. He's driving from Leicester.'

'Mum?'

Oli shoved her on the hip with his stockinged foot.

'Giving Nan moral support at the hospital. She told you this morning, oh bear of little brain.'

'The detached retina. I forgot. Any news?'

'Mum texted. She's got to have an operation.'

'Poor her.'

Oli scrambled to his feet.

'I think it's pretty routine. There's nothing to worry about. They do it while you're still awake.'

'Gross! I can't stand anything to do with eyes.'

'Come and see what I've done for tea.' He laughed. 'Sheep's eye risotto.'

'Oli!'

Jess kicked her shoes into a corner and padded after him. A rich, spicy-sweet aroma filled the house.

'What is it?'

'Oli Hampshire's Chicken and Chorizo Hotpot.'

Jess knew it was somebody else's recipe. Oli would memorise the page of the cookbook, hide it then prepare his food with gusto, pretending he had invented every step himself. He slipped his hands into the oven gloves, thumped the heavy casserole dish onto the hob and lifted the lid. He dipped a wooden spoon into the dish and offered it to her.

'Taste.'

'Mm. That's ... gorgeous.'

And it was, eye-flicker delicious. Oli chuckled.

He took two plates from the cupboard. 'Mum said we should eat. She might stay with Nan for a bit.'

Jess watched him ladling out the hotpot. She cut some bread and opened the fridge.

'No butter?'

'Only that fancy marge.'

'Oh, we're not going healthy again!'

Jess was about to reply when her phone went. It was Eve. Oli could only hear one side of the conversation.

'Don't be silly, Eve. No, I don't think you've been acting weird.'

She glanced at Oli. He was pulling faces. She pulled faces back.

'Honestly, I hardly noticed. No, of course I'm not angry with you. Yes, see you tomorrow. Bye.'

She hung up.

'What's with Eve?' Oli asked.

'She's acting weird.'

He laughed.

'You just said ... !'

'I lied. You can't tell your best friend she's acting weird, even when she is.'

'I always thought Eve was a nice kid, really level-headed.'

That made Jess smile. Kid! Oli wasn't much older than she was.

'She is. It's got something to do with Anthony, I know it.'

Oli questioned her with a look then a one-word question.

'Anthony?'

'He's new. He only started today.'

'So what's Eve got against him? Antennae? Webbed feet and a frog's head? Oh my God, don't tell me, he's . . . a Southerner?'

'I only wish I knew.'

She gave it some thought. Why was Eve so touchy? She mulled it over for a while, but was none the wiser. Eve had always been quite shy with boys, but she had never been like this. It was as if she knew something about Anthony, but how could she? Neither of them had set eyes on him before that day.

'You don't think she's jealous, do you? I've talked to him a couple of times. Do you think that's it?'

Oli pushed back his chair and considered her for a moment.

'I'm afraid I left my mind-reading kit in my room, but it doesn't sound like Eve. She's a generous spirit, especially where you're concerned. She'll tell you when she's good and ready.'

Jess smiled. Oli always seemed older than he was. He was the wisest person she knew, and that included her mother. He cleared his throat.

'I've got some news,' he said. 'I'm going to tell them.'

'Are you sure?'

'Sure as I can be.'

Jess's face was a study of conflicting emotions.

'Are you going to do it tonight?'

'No, over the weekend. There will be more time to talk.'

His words had an immediate impact. Jess laid her palms on the table, fingers spread, and blew out her cheeks.

'There are going to be fireworks. They make out they're pretty liberal and all, but something like this. Who knows?'

'They've got to know sometime. It's better this year, when I'm in Year 12, than next when I'm in the middle of my A levels. You know Mum and Dad. They're bound to freak.'

'Don't you think you're being unfair?'

He grinned.

'You were the one who said there would be fireworks.'

She moved round the table, dropped her arms over his shoulders and leaned her forehead on the back of his head.

'I love you, Oli.'

He laughed.

'Back at you.'

'No, I mean it, you idiot.'

He managed to be serious for at least a minute.

'Don't go sentimental on me, Jess. I'm going to need your support.'

'You've got it always. You know that.'

He squeezed her hands.

'Yes, I know.'

The house was empty when I got home. Six months on, I still hadn't got used to the silence. Once it was full of questions and answers, squabbles, jokes, stories, laughter, all the things that go on in a family home. There were squeals of frustration when a shoe went missing, frantic searches for car keys when somebody was late for work, the tossing of cushions when the remote was nowhere to be found. Such a short time ago there had been four people in this house. Now there were two. Somehow four divided by two wasn't two. It was nothing.

I tugged the key from the lock, pulled out my phone and texted Mum. A message pinged back instantly. She was picking up some shopping. She wouldn't be long. I pocketed the phone and stood for a moment at the bottom of the stairs, gazing at Rosie's portrait. It was Paul who'd painted the block print. It faced you as you entered the house, examined you as you climbed the stairs. I contemplated the impish grin, the small, bright features, the nose stud, the frame of lovingly braided hair. I saw the image every morning as I left the house, every afternoon as I returned. It was the first thing the house told you when you entered. Rosie used to live here. Once, not so very long ago, it rang to the beat of her rhythms, hummed with her earnestness and humour, but not any more. She would never rush out to college. She would never call out that she was home. The portrait told anyone who cared to know that her presence had illuminated this place, but her laughter would never be heard here again. She was gone and we who remained felt her absence like a gnawing pain.

I climbed the stairs, dropping my eyes as I passed Rosie's picture. I crossed the carpeted floor and sat on the window seat opposite the door. It was one of the features that had persuaded my parents to buy the stone cottage overlooking the moors. All the bedrooms had broad wooden window seats. Mum in particular loved the idea of gazing out at the changing seasons on the unspoiled hills. She had grown up in a terrace where the only views had been of a tiny yard and a neighbour's wall. The views answered a lifelong yearning. If you strained your eyes you might make out the white blades of a distant wind turbine. Otherwise the landscape was much as it had been for centuries.

The door went.

'Hi, love.'

'Hi, Mum. You OK?'

She set the shopping down on the floor. Our cats, Jem and Scout, scurried over to investigate, rubbed legs, mewed a greeting and vanished.

'I'm fine. How was school?'

She sensed the hesitation as I jogged downstairs and followed her into the kitchen.

'Eve? Something wrong?'

'No, of course not.'

I grabbed a couple of bags and started putting things away. I could feel Mum's eyes on my back. She wasn't stupid. She knew that haste meant anxiety, but she didn't press me. She knew I would open up in my own good time. That's how it was with us. With Rosie and Dad gone, we had had to create a whole new set of rules.

Slowly, tentatively, we were learning to live differently.

As we unpacked, Mum put a few things to one side: a packet of chicken, garlic, a tin of plum tomatoes, some dried oregano, a packet of fusilli, some chicken stock. She didn't have to say what we were having. We had seven or eight regular meals. I got a couple of bay leaves out of the cupboard, which earned a smile. Mum cut the chicken with a pair of bright turquoise scissors, trimming the white fat. I peeled the garlic and sliced it finely.

Soon the pasta was boiling, steam rising into the hood above the cooker. The garlic sweated in olive oil. Finally, Mum added music to the mix. It was the White Stripes. *Fell in Love with a Girl*. I watched the sauce simmering away and felt a pang. Everybody used to fall in love with Rosie. Then somebody decided to hate her. I stopped, planted my hands on the counter and took a deep breath. It was time to talk.

'There's a new boy in school. Anthony Broad.'

Mum stopped stirring, stiffened and turned in my direction.

'Say that again.'

'Anthony Broad.'

There was no need to check his name. She knew every detail of the case inside out. She did it anyway. She went into the small adjoining room she used as an office. She dropped into her chair and moved the mouse round the pad to wake the computer. She clicked on mail and scrolled through her messages. When she found what she was looking for, she leaned forward. She had received a stream of these emails last August and September, straight after the attack. They'd been sent anonymously from people appalled by what had happened. Most of them fingered the same five boys and a few others who hadn't taken part, but had done nothing to stop them. Mum scanned the list of names. First the attackers. Then she started on the list of onlookers.

'He's there. Anthony Broad.'

Tears spilled down my face.

'I knew it.'

He was there when they attacked Rosie. This new boy, this Anthony Broad, had stood and watched while they beat Rosie and Paul to the ground. He'd done nothing to help them. He was one of the ones who'd watched.

The night Rosie died.

I DO NOTHING

Wednesday, 26 February 2014

It had been three days and what had I done? Anthony Broad was walking the corridors of my school. He wasn't what I had expected. He should have been arrogant. He should have walked with a swagger. But no, he was more like me, one of life's observers. That didn't change anything. His very presence at Shackleton was an insult to Rosie's memory. What was he doing here?

The police said there were people in the park that night.

If anybody on this Earth should have been allowed to live her days in peace it was Rosie. But they came for her. The worst of people dragged down the best. They took her from the world and left it to people like me to fill the aching void.

Jess kept asking if something was the matter. Had she done something to annoy me? Was I upset, depressed? I told her to leave it. Over and over again I told her, no, there was nothing. She didn't believe me. She knew me too well. Then she would drift off to flirt with Anthony, and what did I say? Nothing. What did I do? Nothing. It wasn't Jess's fault she liked him. She didn't know, and I didn't tell her. I was the worst kind of coward. Rosie was my sister and I was unable to summon the courage to confront him. Instead I stood, watching Jess and

Anthony talking, growing closer. All I could do was look on, pleading inwardly for her to come away. But not once did I open my mouth. I felt as if I was killing my sister all over again with my traitor's silence.

Anthony knew her name. It was Eve. Eve Morrison. This was no coincidence. She was the dead girl's sister. He screamed inside. How could this have happened? His mother had planned their flight from Brierley so they could make a new start, untangling herself from her terrifying boyfriend, Roy Mosley, and untangling Anthony from the August night he couldn't forget. They had lived in fear. What if Mosley discovered their bags? What if his snarling, possessive curiosity thwarted their plans?

But they had done it. Mosley hadn't suspected a thing. That should have been it, the happy ending. Now here they were stumbling over another bed of hot coals, squirming on another skewer. Didn't Mum think to check if Rosie had brothers or sisters? Didn't she ask where the Morrisons lived? Maybe he was being unfair. They had fled, hurrying into the street, scrambling into a taxi with their hastily packed belongings while Mosley was out. They had planned for it, prepared for it. Even then, for all that, the last moments of their imprisonment had been raw with terror. They ran, but they hadn't run far enough.

Anthony stood listening to Jess chatting away, but all the while he was flicking anxious glances in Eve's direction. He would never have made the connection with Rosie. Rosie was petite, unforgettable with her dark, alternative clothes and the black hair framing her pale face. She had been like a shadow that night, a shadow with a face like a splinter of moonlight. Eve was taller with a fuller, more rounded face and figure. More importantly, she was conventional, devoted to the idea of blending in with the other girls, a follower rather than a rebel. The longer Anthony looked at her, the less he saw the family resemblance.

'So what is it, yes or no?'

He heard Jess's question as if it had come bubbling through water.

'Sorry. What did you say?'

Jess wasn't annoyed that he had become distracted. She had a sweet personality. Any other time he would have been basking in the attention of this warm, friendly, incredibly fanciable girl. But she hung around with Eve. That meant trouble. Eve was over there now, by the wall, watching them. He found her steady gaze unsettling. Why didn't she ever say anything?

'Are you on Facebook?'

'Oh, no. I don't really do the networking thing.'

There was a good reason. There were things he wanted to forget.

'What have you got against Facebook? I'm always on it. Sometimes I use Twitter.' She cocked her head. 'So what *do* you do? What's Anthony Broad's life like when he's away from school?'

'I read, swim, play my guitar.'

He had her attention.

'You play guitar! Are you in a band?'

'No.' He waited a beat. 'That is, I was.'

'What happened?'

Horror happened.

'I moved. I lost touch with the other guys.'

Jess frowned over her smile. There it was again, the look that said his explanation didn't make sense. Do people really lose touch that quickly?

Anthony knew he would never go back, not for a day, not even for a minute.

Jess waved at Eve to come over, but Eve stayed where she was. Jess waved again, but she got the same response. Eve refused to budge.

'I don't think she likes me,' Anthony said.

'It's not that,' Jess insisted. 'She's kind of shy. You'll like her when you get to know her.'

Anthony didn't see that happening. He knew her behaviour had nothing to do with shyness. It was down to who he was. What he was.

The knock came in the middle of the Art lesson. It was Mr Hudson, one of the Assistant Heads. Jess leaned into me.

'I wonder what that's about? Did you see the look on Anthony's face?'

When I didn't answer, she gave me a nudge.

'Mr Hudson has taken Anthony out of class, Eve. Or didn't you notice?'

'Of course I noticed!'

She didn't react to my raised voice.

'So what's going on?'

My instinctive response was to mumble that I didn't know. Somehow, that was worse than silence. Mrs Carroll was starting to pay attention to us, so I answered in a whisper.

'You tell me. You've been following him around for days.'

'I was trying to be friendly.'

Mrs Carroll didn't think we had got the message so she rose from her seat and wandered around the Art room, ducking under the mobiles dangling from the ceiling. But for her timely intervention we might have launched into a full-scale quarrel.

When the bell went, we followed the throng out into the yard. The Art department was part of a new block that houses Design and Technology, a drama studio and the music rooms. There were posters for a talent show. Predictably, it was entitled *Shackleton's Got Talent*. How original! A sudden shower was sweeping across the school grounds. I hugged my blazer and sprinted over to the main building. Jess followed, her face stung by the whipping rain. She grabbed my sleeve.

'Can't we drop it, Jess?'

'This has got nothing to do with us having words,' she told me. 'I just saw your mum.'

I stopped, suddenly attentive.

'Are you sure?'

At the far end of the corridor, the Head's PA was showing Mum into the waiting room.

I knew Mum would be waiting for me. She waved and Jess and I jogged over. Jess was the first to lean into the open window.

'We saw you earlier.'

'I've been in to see Mr McKechnie.'

Jess heard the note of finality and let it drop.

'Would you like a lift home, Jess?'

Jess gave a kind of shrug, a small sign that she was disappointed to be kept out of the loop, and got in the car. Mum pulled away from the pavement. Nobody said very much. There was the beat of wiper blades and Whitesnake on the sound system. The terraced houses flashed by, the charity shops, hurrying people, the churches, open fields and patches of waste ground. We were soon outside Jess's house, quiet beneath the thunder of the worsening downpour.

'See you tomorrow, Jess.'

'Yes, see you.'

She stood watching us go, her hair already plastered to her face. Before long the grey mist swallowed her and I turned to Mum.

'You went in about Anthony, didn't you?'

The traffic had slowed and we were crawling through the congested High Street. Our entire area is a string of villages and small towns that punctuate the rolling countryside.

'Mr McKechnie had no idea who Anthony Broad was.'

'What's he going to do?'

Mum was concentrating. I remembered how she had

smashed into some bollards the day after the attack. The police had found her clinging to the steering wheel, great, hacking sobs tearing at her.

'He wasn't one of the attackers. He hasn't been charged with anything.'

'He didn't come forward as a witness,' I reminded her, as if she needed any reminding.

'I know, love. He's contemptible, but I discussed it at length with Mr McKechnie. I can't force him to exclude the boy. There are no grounds. He's got a right to an education.'

Something told me that was Mr McKechnie talking, not Mum.

We pulled up outside our house and sat there with the engine idling. Neither of us moved. The rain smeared the windscreen, making the line of the hills sway in the downpour.

'What's going to happen?'

Mum fought to control her voice.

'You won't be in any classes with him. I made sure of that. The situation will be explained to all the teachers.'

'Are they going to say who he is, you know, to the rest of the students?'

I wasn't sure how I felt about that. Did I want everybody to know?

'No. There won't be any big announcement. The school wants to keep a lid on this. I suppose I can understand their attitude. They want to avoid it turning into a point of conflict.'

Part of me wanted exactly that, a peaceful life, no trouble, nobody staring at me and whispering. All those weeks after Rosie died, I'd been a freak, the dead kid's sister. I couldn't walk along the corridor without people stopping and staring.

'Do you think they can?'

Meaning: do you think they *should*?

'Mr McKechnie doesn't want us to make an issue of it.' She started laughing, streams of sadness and bitterness mixing. 'That's what he said. He doesn't want *us* to make an issue of *him* being in school. You'd think Anthony Broad was the victim.'

'What did you say?'

She thumbed her phone and stared at the unread emails.

'Mum, what did you say?'

'I gave him my assurance that we wouldn't cause a scene. Mr McKechnie will make sure you don't have to have any direct contact with Anthony.'

My gaze slipped away. I found myself studying the passers-by struggling with coats, hats, umbrellas, as they battled the wind and rain.

'Eve,' she said. 'There's something else, another reason I don't want this to come out.' She stroked the back of my hand. 'You've had to put up with so much.'

'Why do I know I'm not going to like this?'

'If I can persuade this boy to act as a witness . . .'

'*You're* going to see Anthony?'

'I'm going to see his mother.'

'Did you tell Mr McKechnie?'

She let go of my hand.

'No.'

I THOUGHT YOU KNEW

Saturday, 1 March 2014

Anthony hit the gleaming surface cleanly. The muffled sounds of the world above boomed in his ears. He swam powerfully, ploughing up and down the pool. He was aware of three boys about ten years old, racing along the side and jumping in, gripping their knees. They ignored the sign that said 'No Bombing'. The lifeguard didn't take his eyes off them. Any moment he was going to remind them about the safety rules.

Anthony relaxed into his stroke, gliding through the water, but he was unable to calm his thoughts. They raced. They tormented him. Cartmel Park replaced the shimmering water. Gollum was offering him a can of Coors.

'It'll put hairs on your chest.'

He laughed.

'You need some. Look at this. You've got skin like a girl.'

Gollum didn't mean anything. That was his sense of humour. They'd been mates for years. That's when they saw a gang of lads, roaring and messing around, high on a cocktail of Lambrini, Schnapps and various beers and lagers. Anthony wondered how they were still standing. He wanted to leave, to walk through the windless night and sit in his room, playing his guitar. Anthony didn't know why Gollum even started to talk to them. He loathed them instantly, their sick sense of humour, the way they wanted him to act like them.

'I'm going.'

'Oh, wait a bit, Ant,' Gollum said.

They noticed the couple taking a shortcut through the park.

'Now what have we got here? Look at the moshers.'

Anthony squeezed his eyes shut as he swam. That's how it had started. That was the beginning. He tried to force the stifling August night from his thoughts. Jess took its place. He had been on edge, leaving home to come to the pool. In an unguarded moment he had let it slip that he liked swimming. Jess had seized on the information, asking him when he went. He had been offhand, but Jess was nothing if not persistent. So he had left it as late as possible to make his way to the pool, arriving an hour before it closed. To his relief, it was all but deserted. There had been no time for girls after the incident. Yet there was a wall between him and Jess, one of which she was still ignorant. He had no choice but to keep her at arm's length. A voice echoed suddenly.

'Anthony!'

His heart slammed. He reached the end and turned towards the voice. Jess looked stunning in a sapphire-blue swimsuit. She perched on the side with her feet dangling next to him. He gazed up at her, the light from the glass atrium falling on her face.

'I thought you weren't coming. I was just drying my hair then I decided to take one last look and there you were.'

He made an attempt at humour.

'Here I am. Yay!'

She laughed. How he would have loved to make her laugh more often, but how could he, with what happened to Rosie hanging over him? His smile faded. Jess looked disappointed.

'You should smile more often. It suits you.' She tilted her head. 'What makes Anthony so sad?'

He changed the subject.

'Where's Eve?'

'I came by myself. We're not joined at the hip, you know.'

She tapped his shoulder with her toe.

'I'll see you at the door. You can walk me back.'

J ess was still smiling when she got home. Anthony had started to come out of his shell. He could be charming company when he tried. The smile drained from her face the moment she entered the living room. Oli had his hands laced behind his head. He was leaning back in a not very convincing show of nonchalance while Mum and Dad sat opposite him. The showdown had started without her.

'They think I should stay in the closet,' he said, barely acknowledging her arrival.

His father reacted furiously. 'Neither of us said anything remotely like that! You will not misrepresent us.'

Oli dropped the front legs of the chair back on the floor with a thud.

'Dad, you flipped.'

'I did not flip. I was surprised, that's all. It comes as a bit of a shock when your son tells you he's gay. It came out of the blue. Your mum and I had no idea, did we, Karen?'

She dropped her head.

'Karen?'

'I'm sorry, John.'

The united front between them dissolved in Dad's look of disbelief.

'You mean . . .?'

'I knew. I've known for some time.'

'You never said anything.'

It was hardly an accusation. He was drifting, trying to learn how to steer.

'I thought you knew too. I mean, how could you not?'

Dad leaned closer to Mum and hissed a bewildered complaint.

'Why didn't you say anything? Is that how much I matter in this house?'

'I don't know. It never seemed to be the right time. Maybe somehow I knew it had to come from Oli.'

'It did,' Oli said, coming to her rescue. 'You can't force somebody into the closet. You can't make them come out either.' A sigh. 'Look, I didn't do this to upset anybody. This isn't some kind of teen rebellion. I didn't go, ooh, get a tattoo, be gay, what's it going to be? I didn't set out to shock. I'm setting things straight. I'm telling you what . . . I don't know . . . what I am.' He gave his words a moment's reflection and corrected himself. 'I'm explaining *who* I am.'

He waited for his father to react.

'Dad? Say something.'

The answer was some time coming.

'You are what you are, Oli. God knows, I wasn't expecting this, but it looks like I'm going to have to get used to it.'

'So you're OK with it?'

Everybody in the room heard the question sway like a toddler reaching for the couch, totter, then crash to the floor.

'You can't leave it at that. Come on, Dad.' There was no answer. 'Mum, what about you? Please, anything.'

'Oli, your dad and I love you so much. You're a fine young man and a wonderful son.'

'Is there a "but" coming?'

'There is no "but". Our love for you is unconditional. You know we're not prejudiced. Times have changed, but some people are still so full of hate. At least it's not like the old days. It's going to take some getting used to, that's all.'

'But you're prepared to get used to it? You're not going to freak all the time?'

'We're your mum and dad. You can rely on us. Can't he, John?'

The silence was long enough to be uncomfortable.

'John?'

Then there was a gruff answer.

'Yes.'

I DON'T WANT YOU TO SEE HIM!

Saturday, 1 March 2014

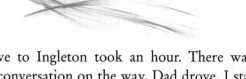

The drive to Ingleton took an hour. There wasn't much conversation on the way. Dad drove. I stared out of the window. Why is it that the more you've got to say, the harder it is to say it? It was as if we had a third passenger, a kind of gremlin who sat between us and pressed his fingers to both our lips.

Mum had her interview with the journalist that afternoon. We had left her arranging the material she wanted to show him, about the attack and its aftermath. She had this engine inside her, driving her on, striving after a truth that always seemed out of reach. Rosie had left a hole in her life. The fight for justice would never fill it, but maybe, if it could go part of the way she would begin to heal or at least learn to live with the pain.

'It's been a while,' Dad said as we pulled into the Broadwood car park and paid the entrance fee to the attendant, who told us the walk would take two to four hours. There were ten waterfalls, a thousand steps. The guy seemed to have a thing with numbers. Dad caught my eye and smiled. We found a parking space.

We set off along the river through Swilla Glen. The thin March sunlight was on the oak, ash and birch, picking out their early spring colours and defining them against the grainy shades of the sky. I climbed quickly over the steep steps.

'Good choice,' I said, glancing back to see him labouring forward. He'd looked better.

'It's good to make the effort,' I said. 'Coming up here beats going to McDonald's and wondering what to talk about.'

That nod again. Dad seemed to register my comments without feeling any desire to answer them. I wouldn't have dared mention McDonald's if Rosie had been there. She detested the brand. She must have protested outside half their restaurants in north-west England. I seem to remember Paul wearing a chicken hat, but maybe that was one of their mates. I never quite got the point of the pickets.

'Isn't that where fathers take their kids when marriages break up?'

'I don't know, love. I'm no expert. Fell in love once. Married once. Long-term relationships – one.'

'So why are you and Mum living apart?'

'I don't think of us as broken up,' he said. 'We just can't live together right now.'

'What's the difference?'

'I don't know.' He considered it for a few moments. 'Doesn't broken up mean there's no love left?'

'So you still love each other?'

He shrugged uneasily. 'Sharp, aren't you? I love her too much to find someone else, but not enough to move back in.'

He snapped open his carrying case and trained the camera lens on the turn of the river. He took some shots and reviewed them with a few flicks of the thumb. Somebody once said that children keep families together. But what about the child who died? Does their loss push families apart? Is grief a blade that saws away at the fraying fibres of love?

We reached Pecca Bridge. Bracken and heather were tossing in the strengthening wind. The clouds were beginning to race, transformed from an ominous blanket to a series of tumbling cascades, mirroring the falls below. Dad took his photographs and gave me one of those uncertain smiles of his.

'The first time we brought you here, you went on strike,' he chuckled.

'What do you mean, went on strike?'

'You said you were tired, so you sat on the ground and refused to go any further. What you didn't realise was that you were plonking yourself down in a puddle. You weren't best pleased.'

'I bet I wasn't!'

'Rosie called you Soggy Knickers all the way to the café.'

'She would!'

I said it with feeling. As if she was still here. As if I could remind her about it. As if . . .

He got me in his viewfinder. I leaned forward so my hair masked my features.

'Don't do that. You've got such a pretty face.'

'No, I haven't!'

'Give me a smile, Eve.'

'Proper photographers don't get you to grin into the lens, Dad. They get you to gaze wistfully into the distance so they can capture your profile.'

I posed by way of illustration; Jane Eyre turning towards Thornfield Hall. That's when he got his photo.

'There you go, Madonna of the Falls.'

'That's cheating!'

'Got your picture though, didn't I?'

He did a little dance, embarrassing dad stuff, but it made me smile all the same. He didn't deserve what had happened. None of us did. The stuff with the camera was the moment that banished the discomfort we felt in each other's company. After that we were able to talk more easily, not that we said much, but when we shared our feelings it wasn't stilted, it wasn't for the sake of it.

Jess wanted to chat about what had happened, and who better to confide in than me? She left it until after eight o'clock. She knew I'd gone out with Dad for the day. Jess was always asking how my mum and dad could have split up. They seemed settled, for keeps, the way the hills are, forever.

'Eve? Great. You're back. How was your day?'

'We went to Ingleton Falls.'

'Where's that?'

'Yorkshire. It wasn't far, an hour's drive.'

'Your dad OK?'

I wasn't sure how to answer at first. I wound up telling her what she wanted to hear.

'Yes, he's fine. You know, getting by.'

Jess was usually a good listener, but she had her own story to tell.

'Eve,' she raced seamlessly into it, 'you won't believe what's happened. Oli's only gone and told Mum and Dad.'

I was still thinking about my own dad, and the burden of sadness he carried.

'What, the big one?'

'Yes, he came right out with it. "Mum, Dad, I'm gay".'

'How did they take it?'

'Mum was fine. Dad kind of flipped. It's not that he's homophobic or anything. I think he's worried about how people are going to react. He says there used to be queer-bashers round here. Grown men used to follow anybody they thought was gay and kick their heads in.

47

Can you imagine it, beating the crap out of a stranger for nothing?'

The question felt like a slap across the face.

'You know what, Jess, I really can.'

Jess heard the mix of hurt and accusation in my voice. She realised instantly what she had said.

'Oh my God, Eve, I'm so sorry. Why don't I think before I open my stupid mouth?'

I didn't rush to reassure her.

'You can't feel what it's like until you've been there. Nobody can.'

'I didn't . . .'

'Look, I'm not angry, Jess.' I had made my feelings known. That was enough. 'Let's not talk about this. You phoned about Oli. Is he OK?'

I could almost hear her scraping together her scattered thoughts.

'Eve . . .'

'Just tell me about Oli.'

There was a moment's silence before she picked up her thread.

'Well, that's the first step taken.'

I wasn't sure what she meant.

'First step?'

'Yes, he's come out to Mum and Dad. What about everybody else?'

'You mean he's going to tell everybody?'

'Can you see Oli staying in the closet now?' Jess said.

I thought about that spiky, confident brother of hers.

'Come to think of it, no.'

'Exactly.'

'Is he worried about how it'll go down at school?'

'He doesn't let on,' Jess said, 'but he's got to be a bit nervous.'

'You tell him I'm there for him,' I said.

I could hear the warmth in Jess's voice.

'He knows, Eve. We both do.'

Sunday, 2 March 2014

I n the flat above the estate agent the bell rang. Anthony looked up. There was an apprehensive glance from his mother.

'You didn't invite anyone round, did you? Somebody you met in school?'

'Of course not.'

'Who knows where we live?'

The reply was instant.

'Nobody.'

But Jess knew. Eve knew. His mother edged to the window and peered through the blinds.

'Mum, who is it?'

'A woman. I don't recognise her.'

His mother glanced down at the street a second time and cursed.

'What?'

'She's seen me. She's started waving.' She thought for a moment. 'She's nothing to do with Roy.' Her breath caught. 'Oh God, I've seen her picture in the papers. It's the girl's mother. I'll have to talk to her.'

Anthony felt a rush of panic.

'Mum, don't!'

The bell shrilled again. He closed the door and sat on

the edge of his bed. His throat was tight. He knew at that moment that the nightmare was never going to end. A few moments later there were footsteps on the stairs and the hinges squeaked. His mother let the stranger in. The woman identified herself. Anthony didn't catch what she said, but he knew Mum was right. It was Eve's mother.

'How did you find us?' she said.

'My daughter's friend got the address from your son.'

'Look, Mrs Morrison, what do you want from me?'

'I want your son to make a statement to the police. There's still time to tell the truth before the case comes to trial. Others have been brave enough to come forward. Why not Anthony?'

Anthony squeezed his eyes shut. No. Dear God, no, not this.

'Anthony told them the truth. He doesn't know anything.'

'I don't believe you. He was in the park that night. The police interviewed him.'

There was a long silence.

'Mrs Broad?'

'I can only tell you what Anthony told the police. He was in the park. Nobody is disputing that. He was there when your daughter arrived with her boyfriend. There was some banter then it started to get ugly. The police must have told you what was in Anthony's statement.' A short breath followed. 'Mrs Morrison, I know what you must have been through.'

That brought a sharp response.

'No, you don't. You can't even imagine.' Anthony imagined the pinched lips, the knuckles whitening with anger and despair. 'I lost a child. Nobody understands what that means, not until it happens to them.'

Anthony heard the breath shudder out of his mother's lungs.

'I'm sorry. That came out wrong. What they did to her was evil.'

'You fight evil, Mrs Broad. You do something about it. That's why I came. Your son can help me get justice for Rosie.'

'He can't. He left before the violence began.'

The words sounded hollow even from Anthony's hiding place in the bedroom.

'I don't believe you. I got emails. They came anonymously, but they said he was still there when the attack on Rosie and Paul started. He saw what they did.'

'And you believe them? Those emails were anonymous. Doesn't that tell you something? This is malicious tittle-tattle.'

'You know better than that. They were scared, the same way you're scared now.'

Anthony tensed. It took a moment for his mother to speak.

'Anthony cooperated fully with the police. They said there was no need to see him again.'

The silence seemed to go on forever before she spoke again.

'You need to understand my position, Mrs Morrison, our position as a family. I separated from Anthony's father some years ago. A while afterwards I met a man in a pub. He was handsome, charming, funny.'

'Where's this going? I don't see what this has got to do with Rosie's murder.'

'Just hear me out. That man was called Roy Mosley.

I made a mistake moving in with him. He wasn't the man I thought he was. He was brutal, manipulative. The relationship became abusive.'

'He hit you?'

Anthony held his breath. He relived every slap, heard Mosley's every snarled threat.

'Me and Anthony, but that wasn't the half of it. Most of the time it wasn't physical violence. It was worse than that. The bruises he inflicted were psychological. He stripped me of any sense of self-worth. Anthony and I never knew when he would fly into a rage. It was like walking on eggshells. We escaped. We finally got away. We can't do anything that might give him a chance of finding us again.'

Something in her words seemed to spur Mrs Morrison on.

'Is your son here? I could speak to him.'

Anthony listened to the tick of the kitchen clock, the gurgle of the central heating.

'Imagine if this had happened to your son, Mrs Broad.'

'I can't. You've got to believe me, I feel for you. It was the most terrible, wicked thing . . .'

'Those are just words. There were people in the park. Why have so few come forward?'

'They were scared, I guess. Just like Anthony and I were with Roy. A matter of weeks after I got involved with Roy, I was desperate to get out.'

Mrs Morrison broke the silence.

'Mrs Broad, I can't persuade you now. You need time to think about what I've said to you.'

'Anthony can't help the police any more than he already has.'

'We'll see. This is my number. Call me any time, night or day. I want justice for Rosie. I want those animals put away so they can't hurt anyone else. Please.'

'You've been through a terrible torment. So have I. We're on the run. We're in fear of our lives.'

'There's only one way to stop these sort of people. You won't have peace while they walk free. You have to bring them to justice.'

'That's exactly it. You think Anthony saw more than he did. He left the park before a blow was struck. You must believe me.'

'Anthony can help the police. I know he can. Think about it. I will call again.'

'There's no point.'

'You've got my number.'

That was the last thing Anthony heard before the footsteps on the stairs and the slam of the outside door. He started to sob loudly, his chest rising, falling, convulsing, tears spilling down his cheeks.

HAPPY NOW?

Monday, 3 March 2014

I t started when we saw Anthony walking into Mrs Christie's room for registration.

'So it's definite,' Jess said. 'He's been moved. It's because of your mum, isn't it? What's going on, Eve?'

I remembered the state Mum was in when she got back from talking to Anthony's mother.

'Just leave it, OK?'

The argument continued into registration.

'I will not leave it.' She tugged at my sleeve. 'We're supposed to be friends. Are you going to tell me what you've got against Anthony?'

'Jess, I can't.'

'I'll ask Mrs Rawmarsh what's happening.'

Jess raised her arm. She was determined. I made a grab for her, but she shrugged my hand away.

'Miss, where's Anthony?'

Mrs Rawmarsh stared past Jess, at me. That only fed Jess's curiosity.

'He was in our set. Why's he been moved?'

I was aching for Jess to drop it, but the more I ducked her questions, the more determined she became.

'Jess, he has moved to another tutor group. Sometimes we put students in a form temporarily. We move them once they've settled in.' The next sentence was clearly an afterthought. 'It's a numbers thing.'

Not for the first time, Mrs Rawmarsh was looking my way. After a few moments she consulted the sheets of paper on the table in front of her.

'There are just a few notices this morning. Anyone going to Martendale for Year 11 football should see Mr Hurst. He has the transport details. You've got to have your permission slip back by end of school tomorrow. Auditions for *Shackleton's Got Talent*.'

Loud guffaws and catcalls engulfed her. She stared down the disruption. She was Head of Music and the competition was her baby.

'Auditions for *Shackleton's Got Talent* are lunchtime in Music Room A.'

The announcement triggered groans. When they subsided Mrs Rawmarsh shook her head and waved her charges away.

'Off you go, people,' she said, 'and you two . . .' She pointed at Jake and Connor, the pair who had greeted the announcements with mocking laughter. 'Try not to drag your knuckles on the floor, gentlemen.'

I didn't stay to hear their reply. I was chasing Jess down the corridor.

'Where are you going?'

'To see Anthony.'

'Jess, don't. Please.'

'Tell me why not.'

What could I say? Why the hell couldn't Anthony go away?

'Well?'

Mum would never forgive me if I did anything to

prevent Anthony making a statement to the police. I dropped my arms by my side in a helpless gesture.

'OK, I'm going.'

'Jess . . .'

But she was already out of sight.

Anthony heard the opening chords of *Don't Dream It's Over* and stopped by the music room door. He found himself peering inside. He recognised the guitarist from his new tutor group and darted back, hoping he hadn't been seen, but the boy spoke.

'It's Anthony, right?'

'Yes.'

'I'm Charlie.'

'I know.'

Charlie tossed the guitar away in disgust.

'What's up? Having difficulties?'

'I was going to play it in the auditions,' Charlie said. 'Can't get the damned thing right.' He laughed. 'I've tried sticking my tongue out and everything.'

Anthony warmed to him.

'I don't think that really helps.'

'Tell me about it. My tongue's aching and I'm still playing bum notes.'

Anthony held out a hand. He perched on a tall stool and started to fine-tune the guitar.

'Does this mean you play?' Charlie asked.

'A bit. You're rushing it. Try to stay loose. Listen.' Should he be doing this? 'I'll show you if you like.'

Charlie listened as Anthony played.

'Hey, that's perfect. What are you performing in the auditions? You'll blow them away.'

Anthony ran his fingers down the strings.

'I'm not here for the auditions. I was just passing.'

'You should go in for it. Straight up, you're good.'

'I don't have my guitar.'

Charlie gestured to the one in his hands.

'You can use mine. The state of my playing, I'm not going through.'

Anthony felt a rush of panic. The last thing he needed was something drawing attention to him. He had to go before people started to arrive.

'No, I can't. I'm not prepared.'

'Something tells me you don't need much preparation. You in a band?'

'Was. Look, I've got to go.'

The room was filling, blocking his escape. People were arriving for the auditions. Charlie waved his hand in the air.

'Hey, listen to this guy play. Go on, Anthony. Show them.'

Anthony shook his head and started to climb down from the stool.

'Oh, come on. Show everybody what you can do.'

Some of the others joined in.

'Yes, show us what you've got.'

'You can't go now. Charlie's whetted our appetite.'

'Play us something.'

Anthony wavered. It was at this moment that Mrs Rawmarsh arrived.

'What's going on here, guys?'

'We're trying to get Anthony to play. He's really good.'

'Anthony?'

He felt like a fish on a hook.

'Look, I'm really not.'

'Let me be the judge of that.'

Anthony was still searching for an escape route when

he saw Jess drift in from the yard. She looked surprised to see everybody crowding around him. The kid on the edge was suddenly at the centre of things.

'Well,' Mrs Rawmarsh said, 'let's hear you. Somebody's got to get things rolling.'

Anthony protested for a moment or two then settled back on the stool and started to play. There were nods of approval as he went through the opening chords, and broad smiles when he started to sing.

'Well, you're definitely through,' Mrs Rawmarsh said, 'only you might want to pick something more up to date for the real thing!'

Anthony nodded, handed Charlie the guitar and made for the door. Jess put a hand on his chest as he tried to make his escape.

'Well done you!' she cried.

'Thanks.'

'Don't run off,' she said. 'I'm going to listen to the rest. Why don't you stay?'

Her hand was still on his chest. A voice told him to go, leave, get away. No good was going to come of this.

'Please don't go.'

Her eyes were dazzling. Her touch was warm.

'OK, you've persuaded me.'

Jess smiled.

'Cool.'

Jess left the performance and headed for the assembly hall. Why did Eve have to be so stubborn? Was she jealous of Anthony? Was that it? That didn't make sense though. Eve had been hostile from the very beginning. Then there was the way Mrs Morrison had turned up at school before Anthony was moved. It couldn't be coincidence. Jess sat next to Eve in the hall. They'd been friends for years. They weren't going to fall out over it.

'Are we speaking?' she asked.

'Of course. What makes you ask?'

Jess didn't like Eve shutting her out, but what could she do? Mr McKechnie walked to the front.

'Thank you for coming to order so quickly,' Mr McKechnie began. 'As you know, we have reached the semi-final of Shackleton's Great Debate.'

Jess had her gaze fixed on Oli. He had made it to the last four speakers. She could tell he was nervous, playing with his hair, brushing bits of probably imaginary fluff from his knees. Seeing him up there, looking anxious and vulnerable, made her heart go out to him.

'The subject for the final stages, the semi-final and the final is: Has political correctness gone too far?'

Oli caught Jess's eye and she gave him an encouraging smile. The first two speakers didn't seem to say that much. Though they were on opposite sides of the debate, they both seemed to spend most of their speeches explaining what political correctness was rather than saying anything about it. Connor gave a loud yawn that earned him a disapproving glare from the staff. Next up however was Simon Gore, an opinionated sixth former who seemed to revel in setting himself apart from his peers.

'Here he is,' Jess said, grimacing, 'Gore the bore.'

Simon was anything but boring this time. He cut straight to the chase, launching a withering attack on rules that, in his opinion, curtailed free speech.

'Everybody has rights,' he said as he got into his stride. 'Nobody has responsibilities. If you say there is too much immigration you're racist. If you call a girl "love" you're sexist. If you comment on somebody liking the Pet Shop Boys or Judy Garland, you're homophobic.'

Some members of the audience swapped frowns. What *was* he on about?

'They talk about Islamophobia and say Muslims are the victims of attacks. They don't say most of those attacks are verbal, not physical.'

There was a snort of protest from Shabina Begum.

'There you go. If you don't like what I say, you try to shout me down.'

Shabina rolled her eyes.

'Shabina didn't shout,' Jess protested. 'He's being ridiculous.'

Eve shrugged.

'He's getting a reaction. I think that's his plan.'

Encouraged by the interruption, Simon pressed on. 'Well, I say, sticks and stones may break my bones, but words will never hurt me. The moment you start telling people what to say or think, you are on the road to dictatorship. Fascists and communists ban free speech. I say democracy is about the right to offend people. If somebody says something you don't like, don't whine about it. Don't go running to the council. Stand up for yourself. It's a free country. If we put up with political correctness gone mad, it won't be free for much longer!'

Simon Gore wasn't the most popular boy in school, but he sat down to strong applause. Oli was the last speaker.

'I think Simon overstates his case,' he said. 'Laws against discrimination are about protecting people from prejudice. It is ridiculous to say it leads to communism and fascism. Nobody wants to interfere with anybody's free speech.' He seemed to falter. 'But bigotry is real and so is prejudice. Stephen Lawrence was murdered because he was black. Mosques and Islamic schools have been fire-bombed. Violence against women is common.' There was another moment's hesitation. 'Some of us provoke hostility because of our sexual orientation.'

There were a couple of giggles. You didn't hear the word sex in assemblies, any more than you heard tit, bum or fart. Jess was sure the snorts of derision came from Connor and Jake. Mr McKechnie faced them down with an icy stare. Connor was now on his second warning.

'Yes, some of my friends already know, but I am going to say this before all of you. This week I told my parents that I am gay. I am proud of the way I am, as all of you should be of the way you are. So I want to say that all of us at Shackleton, male or female, black or white, straight or gay, have the same right to respect. To oppose prejudice and discrimination is not an attack on free speech. It is not "political correctness gone mad". It is a necessary protection of the rights of all citizens regardless of colour or creed, gender or sexual orientation.'

There was a moment's silence before a few murmurs broke out. Then there was a louder, warmer ripple of applause. Jess looked along her row. A few faces were turned her way.

There was a 'no way' and a couple of whispers of 'you kept that quiet'.

The rest were hard to read. Oli returned to his seat while Mr McKechnie stepped forward.

'Thank you Oliver and thank you to all our other speakers. You will all receive a voting form in the next few days. Two speakers will be eliminated, leaving our finalists to fight it out in a few days.'

As everybody filed out, Jess noticed Jake and Connor staring at her.

'What?'

'Nothing much,' Jake said, 'just that we never had your brother down as a shirtlifter. Don't tell me you're a lez.'

'The way you're always with Eve,' Connor chuckled, 'makes you think.'

Jake leered. 'Can I watch?'

Jess's cheeks were burning. She snarled her defiance.

'One of your fantasies, is it? Get a life, you pathetic moron.'

She suddenly started to struggle against the human tide flowing out of the hall and battled her way through to where Oli was standing talking to his friends. In front of maybe half of her fellow students and the remaining teachers, she hugged him. He laughed.

'What's that for?'

She had tears in her eyes.

'For being the best.'

'Anthony's walking it.'

I did a double take, suddenly aware of Jess waiting for me to reply.

'Sorry, what did you say, Jess?'

'Daydreaming again?' Jess asked. 'You're always away in your own little world lately. I said that Anthony's the best in the competition. Anyway, do you want to do something this evening?'

'Sorry,' I said. 'I've got homework to finish.'

Jess rolled her eyes.

'Eve, at your age you're not supposed to sit at home moping.'

'Is that what you think I'm doing?' I demanded. 'Moping? Jess, moping is what you do when you lose a favourite possession or your puppy is sick. I'm trying to get over a murdered sister.'

Jess was sorry, but not horrified at herself the way she had been the last time we'd talked about it.

'It wasn't the best choice of words, but life goes on.' She saw that I was trying to interrupt. 'No, please Eve, you're my best friend. I love you to bits. Hear me out.' She checked nobody was eavesdropping and whispered the rest. 'I'm not being callous. You can't bury yourself with her. If you give up, those thugs haven't just taken Rosie away. They've destroyed you and your whole family. Eve, you've got to go on living.'

People were moving.

'Look, it's my stop. I'll call you. Think about it, yeah?'

BEING ALIVE IS A STATEMENT

Saturday, 3 August 2013

Rosie made quite an entrance. The front door crashed shut then she appeared in the garden where we were sunbathing.

'Oh, that's why there's a draught. You've got the wind roaring through the house. The door nearly took my hand off.'

I was in the back with Jess, Hannah and Rehana. Hannah hadn't met Rosie before.

'Great look,' she said. 'Love the hair.'

Rosie pinched her dreads, dangling them in front of her face.

'Really? You like them?'

She sounded almost disappointed, as if attracting praise wasn't the point.

'I like the combination of scarlet and black. If it was all one colour it wouldn't look quite so dramatic.'

Rosie smiled and swept back into the house. Dramatic was good.

'So your sister's a goth?'

'Kind of. No, not really. She's *alternative*.'

'What's the difference?'

'She's alternative to everything. She turned up at the goth weekend in Whitby in punk gear.'

'Have you never wanted to copy her?' Rehana asked.

I can honestly say the idea had never occurred to me.

'What, because we're sisters? When we were growing up I wanted to look like Cheryl Cole. She preferred Countess Bathory.'

'Who?'

I gave my fingers a spooky wriggle.

'The Blood Countess. She bathed in the blood of maidens to keep herself young.'

'You're making it up!'

I shook my head. There was a synchronised turn towards the kitchen where Rosie was washing our dishes. She paused and pushed the window open with soapy fingers.

'Don't you ever clean up after youself, Eve? You shouldn't leave everybody else to do it. I don't even live here any more and I do my bit.'

Scout came padding along the windowsill. Jem mewled somewhere out of sight.

'OK, so what are you looking at?'

'I told them about the Blood Countess,' I explained.

Rosie pulled a face.

'I'm done with maidens. I'm moving on to traffic wardens.'

I stifled a yawn and rolled onto my stomach, the sun closing my eyes like invisible fingertips on my lids. I was used to Rosie's weird sense of humour. Rehana and Hannah weren't sure what to make of her.

'Is it a statement?' Hannah asked. 'You know, your look.'

Rosie laughed. 'It's a revolt.'

'Against?'

'Whaddya got?'

Hannah frowned and whispered, 'What's she talking about?'

'It's a movie reference,' I said.

Rosie nodded. '*Wild One* with Marlon Brando.'

There were looks of confusion all round.

'Don't worry about it. It's really old.'

'Black and white?' Rehana asked. 'I don't watch black and white films.'

'Rosie does. She's at MMU, studying Film and Media Studies.'

'What year?'

'Just going into my third,' Rosie answered. 'I graduate next year.'

'So you're into *Twilight* and all that stuff?'

Rosie wrinkled her nose. 'That's gothic lite. I need more darkness, more blood, more *edge*.'

Rehana checked the time on her phone. 'We'd better phone a cab.'

Mum leaned through the kitchen window.

'Don't do that. I'll run you home. Call it Morrison's taxi service.'

'So is it?'
   Rosie tilted her head to one side, squinting against the late afternoon sunlight.

'Is what what?'

'What Hannah said, is this a statement?'

In the golden halo of the fading day Rosie was stunning. Her bodice was lacy, her pale arms bare, her skirts wide and long, almost hiding the black, pointy-toed boots.

'Eve, being alive's a statement.'

'That isn't really an answer, is it?'

'What do you want, Eve? You usually go with the flow.'

'I wondered why you have to be different, that's all.'

'You've never asked before.'

'I'm asking now.'

'Is this because your friends were so curious about me?'

'I suppose. I never really gave it much thought until now. Then I started to see through their eyes.'

'Because I don't fit into their idea of femininity? I don't go for the same uniform.'

She plucked a blade of grass and tickled the tip of my nose.

'Eve, you're funny, you know that? We all belong to some kind of tribe.'

'I don't.'

'Yes, you do. Remember last week? You, Jess and Rehana were all wearing kimono dresses and wedges. What's that?'

She had me, but I wasn't about to give in that easily.

'Coincidence.'

'Mm, a coincidence that you all looked at the same page of the same catalogue.'

I was starting to find the tickling annoying and brushed her hand away. She was sounding smug.

'I've seen you in town with your friends. You all think you're so individual, but you're wearing a uniform too, don't tell me you're not. At least we're not trying to provoke anybody.'

'Neither am I. Neither is Paul. This is me. Take me or leave me.'

I gazed at her for a moment, doing my best to keep my face stern and serious, then the act dissolved and I leaned forward to hug her.

'OK, you can be in any tribe you want, goth girl.'

'You too, fashion chick.'

And we held that embrace for several moments. I just wish I could hold her now.

FRIENDS FOREVER

Wednesday, 5 March 2014

Anthony left his guitar in Music Room 1. Mrs Rawmarsh locked the door and walked across the yard with him.

'It's good to see you joining in more,' she said.

Charlie was lounging against the wall opposite, waiting for him.

'You've made a friend, I see.'

'We're into the same music.'

He noticed something, a hesitation.

'There's a reason for this conversation, isn't there, Miss? There's something bothering you.'

Mrs Rawmarsh ran a hand through her hair.

'You seem to be close to Jess Hampshire.'

'That wasn't meant to happen.'

'There was a good reason for moving you into another form. She's Eve Morrison's best friend. Is this going to be a problem?'

'I don't want to cause any trouble.'

'Just be sensible, Anthony. It might be an idea to keep your distance if you can.'

He watched her striding across the yard.

'What was that about?' Charlie asked.

'She was catching up,' Anthony lied, 'asking me how I was settling in.'

That was his life, half-truth upon half-truth, lie upon lie. It was bound to come out sometime. Part of him wanted to get it over with. Surely anything had to be better than this limbo. Before long Jess appeared with Eve.

'Let's go the other way,' Anthony said.

Once they were round the corner of the sports hall, Charlie tugged at his sleeve.

'Are you crazy? Why do you want to give Jess the slip? If the sexiest girl in Year 11 had the hots for me, I'd let her find me. I'd roll a red carpet right to her feet. Man, I'd give both arms to be where you are.' Charlie rolled his eyes. 'I can't figure you out sometimes.'

'There's nothing to figure out.'

Charlie gave him a shove.

'You sure you haven't got hidden depths?'

Anthony shoved him back.

'No, more like hidden shallows.'

Jess was trying to pretend she hadn't seen Anthony duck round the corner. She started talking fast, about anything, about nothing, rushing out the words so she didn't choke on them, but Anthony's deliberate escape had upset her. I wondered whether maybe this was the best way out. What if he didn't really like her? Then I wouldn't have to tell her what was going on, not until I had to. Oh please, that would solve everything. For now.

'You can drop the act, Jess. I saw him. He couldn't get away fast enough.'

A friend's instinct is normally to say nothing. But these weren't normal times.

'He couldn't have made it more obvious.'

Jess crumpled, her chin quivering.

'What's he playing at? On Monday he seemed to want to be with me.' Her voice faltered. 'It's whenever he sees me next to you.'

But if I thought it was going well, I was fooling myself. Her eyes flashed suddenly.

'This isn't about me at all, is it? There's something between you two. I know it.'

This time it was my defences that were down.

'Don't be stupid. I'd never set eyes on him until a week ago.'

She searched my face.

'I'm not stupid, Eve. You're keeping something from me, both of you. The way you reacted that first day, the way your mum came into school and got him moved . . .'

I could hear doors opening in her mind. Up to this point she had been tangled up in her own interests, her curiosity about Anthony, her concern about Oli. Now, for the first time, her thoughts had broken free of all that. They were racing. It was only a matter of time before she started to make the connection.

'You need to talk to me, Eve. Friends don't keep secrets.'

'Jess,' I pleaded, 'I need you to be patient. Don't press me, please. Just stay away from Anthony.'

'Why?' she cried. 'What's he done that's so terrible . . .?'

Her voice broke off.

'Jess, no.'

Her eyes were wild. In that moment she knew, not the details, but the heart of it.

'Brierley.'

'What?'

'He said he was from Brierley.' There was a moment's pause. 'It's got something to do with Rosie, hasn't it?'

I didn't even try to deny it. Pandora's box was open and the lid could not be closed. The demons were flying. Jess would have gone after Anthony then, confronted him face to face, but the bell rang. I seized her by the arm.

'Listen,' I said. 'Listen to me. We'll find somewhere at break. I'll tell you who he is. Don't do anything until then. Promise.'

She was still drawing away from me.

'Jess, you're my best friend. Maybe I haven't been fair to you, but trust me. Please.' The first fury had gone out of her. I seized the opportunity. 'You don't go near him

82

until I've had a chance to explain. Jess, you've got to give me that.'

The tension was draining away.

'OK. OK, I'll hear you out.'

We headed for the benches overlooking the sports pitches. It was dull and overcast and we shivered in our thin blazers. There was only one thing in favour of the weather. It kept everyone else away from this exposed part of the school grounds. The wind boomed over the fields and clawed through the chain-link fencing.

'I was right, wasn't I?' Jess demanded. 'He was there the night Rosie was attacked.'

There was no point denying it.

'He was there.'

'Oh God!'

'I had to keep quiet about it. Mum thinks he might act as a witness.'

'After all this time?'

'I think she's clutching at straws. After everything that's happened I'm not sure she trusts the law to do its job. She just wants justice to be done.'

We huddled together.

'Somehow I don't see Anthony as a thug,' Jess said. 'Are you sure you've got this right? What did he do? How much did he see?'

How many times had I asked the same question? I kept re-running the possible scenarios through my mind. In some he fled the park almost immediately. In others he watched, fascinated, as they swarmed around Paul and Rosie. I even imagined him lashing out like the rest of them.

'We only know what those anonymous emailers told us. They all say he wasn't involved in the attack, but he was there.' I struggled to finish what I was saying. Just talking about it made my eyes sting and my voice choke off. 'It's complicated.'

'Complicated how?'

'Mum went to see him. Well, she went to see his mum.'

'You're kidding! Is she allowed to do that?'

I shrugged. 'She did it anyway. You know what she's like. She's still fighting for Rosie. She said Anthony's mum seemed scared.'

Jess sighed.

'You're right. What a mess.' She took my hand. 'So what happens now?'

'We stay away from him.'

'I don't know if I can do that. Not when he pretended to be something he wasn't.'

'Please.' We were both trembling. 'No matter how much you want to shout and scream, we do nothing. If there is a chance he will come forward as a witness, we can't do anything to put it at risk. Mum would never forgive me.'

The bell shrilled in the distance.

'Still friends?' I asked.

Jess smiled.

'Friends forever.'

Memories are razors. Dreams are instruments of torture. Thoughts come swarming like wasps, leaving their poison burning in your flesh. When you lose a sister, it is not an end, but the beginning of your understanding of her. You know her better, need her more, but she is no longer there. Her absence is the ultimate wound.

Anything can bring her walking back through the door, a holiday photograph, a scent, a taste, a memento gathering dust on a shelf or nestling in a packing case. With me, it was music, not the kind you expect. It wasn't Evanescence or Marilyn Manson that brought Rosie back into my heart. It wasn't the stuff that formed a soundtrack to her life. It was a band called Fun, not the kind of music she usually listened to at all, and a song called *We Are Young*. The first time I heard it, a few weeks after the attack, it owned me. Rosie would never grow old. Age would not weary her. The years would not condemn. I would remember her forever, twenty years old, beautiful and doomed.

That is how the pain begins. For hours, maybe even days, I put her in a gallery in my mind. For however short a time I think I can leave her there, to be brought out from time to time when I am ready to face her, but it isn't like that at all. Just when I am least expecting it, she is there beside me. I feel the brush of an arm, hear a ripple of laughter, share a common experience. But here is the turn of the screw, the burn of the brand. When I go to speak to her, when I want to embrace her and share a secret, she is gone, swept away like leaves in an autumn breeze.

She has to return to the shadows, shrink back into the photos and videos, be confined in objects and bric-a-brac. I phoned Jess that night about half past eleven and we talked. I tried to explain all this. The last thing I said would later come back to haunt us both.

'No matter how close we were in life, I can never have said I love you enough. We can never have done all the things together we should have. Jess, you have to treasure every moment you have with Oli and your mum and dad. Hold them. Fight for them. Because life is much more fragile than you think.'

I SOUNDED LIKE ROSIE

Thursday, 6 March 2014

Something had changed.

Anthony had caught Jess's eye two or three times now. On each occasion she had looked away, but this wasn't flirting. Her eyes were dull. Gone was the spark that lit her gaze whenever she saw him. This was contempt, even disgust. Anxiety clawed at him. Had Eve finally told her? Was he about to be exposed before the whole school?

It didn't add up. If she knew, why hadn't she confronted him? There had been no repercussions, no pointing finger, no rumours, no accusations. Instead there were these cold stares.

'What are you going to play in *Shackleton's Got Talent*?' Charlie asked, breaking into Anthony's thoughts.

'No idea.'

'You've got to be joking. The final is next week. How can you not know?'

'I've listened to hours of music. Nothing seems quite right.'

'Do you want to do this?'

Anthony didn't duck the question.

'You want an honest answer? No. I mean, the whole thing got sprung on me. I was happy the way I was.'

Charlie cocked his head. Anthony had struck a false note.

'I know happy, Anthony, and you weren't it.'

There was a moment's silence.

'You were in a band. You must enjoy the limelight from time to time. You just said you've spent hours searching for something to play.'

Anthony nodded.

'So play.'

'It isn't as easy as that. It has to be the right song. I've got to feel it.'

As if he had felt anything but fear since his mother met Mosley. Since then, life had been a series of humiliations.

'Well, you'd better find something, my friend, and fast.'

Voting on the Great Debate was in full swing.

Jess was next to me, staring at the display board outside the dining hall.

'Oli's got it in the bag,' she observed. 'Everybody says he was the best.'

'He'll get to the final,' I said, 'but I don't think it's a foregone conclusion.'

'Why not?'

'There are what, three hundred students in Key Stage Four? Do you really think Connor Hughes and Jake Lomas are the only Neanderthals around the place?'

'No, maybe not, but they've got to be in a minority.'

'OK,' I said, 'you think the battle against prejudice is won? We get lessons and assemblies on equal opportunities. Everybody pretends to be all PC. Are you telling me you've never heard a racist or sexist joke? You've never heard the boys comparing the girls' boobs?'

Jess stared at me for a moment, then snorted with irrepressible laughter.

'What's wrong with you?' I demanded, annoyed that my big moment had fallen flat.

'Oh, don't get angry,' she said, squeezing my arm. 'You were so earnest. Honestly, it didn't sound like my Eve. That's the longest speech I've ever heard you make.'

'It wasn't a speech!'

'Yes, it was. You sounded exactly like . . .'

Her voice trailed off.

'Don't worry,' I told her. 'I know what you're thinking. I sounded like Rosie.'

Anthony and Charlie were by the bollards up the road from the school. Anthony was in no hurry. He was walking through the streets and everyone he saw was a statue, still, frozen in time by some Medusa stare. As he continued through the school gates he heard a slow, sinister, cracking sound. Stone heads were turning, chips of grey cascading to the ground. Their eyes were blank the way they were in a museum. Then something happened. From the statues' tear ducts dark, gluey, crimson blood bubbled and spilled in streams down the inanimate faces. Anthony let out a small gasp at the memory.

'Something wrong?'

Charlie was watching him, a frown hardening his usually soft features.

'No, just thinking.'

'You do a lot of that.'

A smile mixed with a nod of the head.

'Yes, that's me, the thinker.'

'Anyway, here's my lift. We're going to the Snow Zone in Manchester. I would have invited you, only we can't squeeze anybody else into the car. Sisters, eh? My parents had to have three of them.'

He walked to the car. He was trying to hold a tune. It was vaguely familiar.

'Charlie,' Anthony said. 'What's that you're humming?'

'*We Are Young.* It was a hit a couple of years back.'

'Yes, I remember it.'

Charlie paused by the car.

'I heard it around school today. Can't think where.' He

rummaged in his memory for a moment. 'No, it won't come.'

'It's not important,' Anthony said.

He was wrong. Charlie had heard it that morning when one of the girls walked past him on the way to registration.

It was Eve Morrison.

Mum was home when I got back. She was sitting in front of the computer screen, screwing up her eyes at the message on the screen. Black Sab's *Paranoid* provided the background noise. Tony Iommi's guitar was ripping through the house.

'Nothing like a bit of Ozzy,' Mum said.

'You'll have the neighbours knocking. What's for tea?'

'Chilli lemon tuna, broccoli and spaghetti. Everything OK at school?'

What was I supposed to say?

'Not bad.' I wanted to tell her the truth, but the old platitudes tripped off my tongue so easily. I changed the subject. 'Oli got his first bit of abuse today.'

'What happened?'

'I heard about it second-hand. Jess said he had a run-in with a couple of boneheads from my form.'

'Who are they?'

'Jake Lomas, Connor Hughes.'

'Hughes? Not Brian Hughes' son?'

'I don't know. Who's he?'

'Runs a scrappie in Martendale. I went to school with his sister.'

I heard the change in her voice.

'I'm guessing this Brian Hughes isn't your kind of people.'

'If it's the same family, I'd tell Oli to steer well clear. Were you there when a bunch of yobs turned the peace stall over?'

I remembered. Mum and Dad used to campaign against

the wars in Iraq and Afghanistan, getting people to sign petitions. Rosie and I would tag along sometimes. Once in a while thugs would try to break up the protest. They'd come out of nowhere that afternoon, five or six burly men, mostly shaven-headed. To the little girl I was then they were like giants. I didn't understand any of it. All I knew was that there was all this rage exploding around me. While Rosie yelled at them, all I could do was scream and dissolve into tears.

'That was him?'

'That was Brian Hughes. He was into the neo-Nazi skinhead scene back then, Skrewdriver and all that. They used to have Blood and Honour gigs at the Wishing Well.'

'On the Blackburn Road?'

'That's the one.'

There wasn't much more to say so I changed the subject.

'Have you heard anything from Anthony's mum?'

'Not yet. If I don't hear by Saturday, I'm going round.'

'Are you sure?'

There was no answer. Her mind was made up.

'I'll crack on with the tea, Eve.' She paused in the doorway. 'But be careful. If this Connor is Brian Hughes' son, he could be trouble.'

HAVE YOU EVER KISSED A BOY?

Thursday, 6 March 2014

It was the final of the Great Debate. It was down to Oli and Simon Gore. There were posters around the school with photographs of both of them. There was a line of kids leaning against the wall opposite the entrance to the hall, maybe twenty in all.

'What's that about?' I asked.

'Their parents have asked them to be withdrawn. Oli says one boy in his class wants to attend, but his dad thinks the school is advertising homosexuality.'

I laughed out loud. 'What, like cereal?'

'Absolutely. Didn't you know? A ninety-second jingle can actually turn you gay overnight.'

I faked a look of dismay. 'No!'

Jess was having fun.

'A little jingle every day is guaranteed to make you gay.'

Hannah gave her daggers.

'Hey, knock it off. This is meant to be serious.'

'Why's it serious? You giggled all the way through Sex Ed.'

'That's different.'

'How's it different?'

'That was boy-girl. It's a laugh. This is boy-boy.'

I interrupted.

'Don't forget girl-girl.'

'You're being stupid,' Hannah objected. 'You know what I mean.'

Jess was suddenly serious.

'No, I don't actually.'

'Look, I'm not prejudiced, but . . .'

Jess shook her head.

'Oh, for God's sake! That's how every bigot starts a sentence.'

'I am not a bigot!'

'So what are you saying?'

'You've got to explain the issues properly.'

I stepped in before Jess lost it.

'There are issues, as you put it, whether you're straight or gay. What's the difference?'

Hannah was slipping into a sulk. Jess softened her attitude.

'Hey, I don't want to beat you up about this. Honestly, Oli feels the same as you do, or Eve or I do, only about other boys.'

Hannah nodded.

'Fine.' Which said it wasn't really fine. 'I didn't mean to hurt your feelings.'

'You didn't.'

I watched them hug. That got Connor's attention.

'See, it's spreading.'

Jess spun round, her face taut with anger.

'It'll never spread as far as you, you sick, sad loser. If I was looking for a boyfriend I'd choose the fattest man on Earth over you. I'd choose road-kill over you.' She jabbed a finger at him. 'Oli told me what you said.'

'Truth hurts, does it?'

Mrs Rawmarsh put a stop to the quarrel.

'Over here, Connor. I want a word.'

'Why me? She started it.'

She wasn't impressed.

'Just how old are you?' No answer. 'I heard every word, Connor. Consider yourself on a warning. One more outburst and you've got yourself an hour's internal exclusion.'

'This sucks. Why are you taking her side?'

'I'm not. You have been provoking the other students for at least two days.'

'You talking about that poof Oli Hampshire?'

'You're walking on thin ice, Connor.'

Mr Hudson had overheard the exchange. He was making his way over. Mrs Rawmarsh gave a little shake of the head to tell him she could deal with it.

'You're always jumping in on their side,' Connor snarled, 'her and her brother.'

'I would advise you to stop there. Absolute silence, young man, or Mr Hudson will remove you and you will spend the next hour outside his room.'

Connor considered his options for a few moments then made a tactical retreat.

'Thank you. Now go back to your place.' Mrs Rawmarsh folded her arms and looked along the line. 'This is going to be a serious debate. I trust nobody else is going to try to turn it into a pantomime.'

Mr Hudson chaired the session.

'Today's final will consist of two rounds. Each speaker will have five minutes to summarise his arguments from the semi-final then there will be a question and answer session before the final vote.'

There was nothing new in either speech. Everybody was waiting for the Q&A. The first question was directed at Oli.

'Why've you got to go on about being gay all the time? It isn't that big a deal.'

Oli was patient.

'I'm not going on about it. It was one part of my presentation.'

'It's the bit everybody remembers,' the questioner retorted.

'Fine, I'll give you a straight answer.'

There were snorts of laughter.

'There are gay people in every community. You're right. It isn't as big a deal as in the old days, and it shouldn't be an issue at all, but there is still a lot of prejudice against LGBT people . . .'

'Against what?'

'LGBT stands for lesbian, gay, bisexual and trans-gender people. I should have explained that.'

There were a few giggles at 'transgender'.

'What, men who dress up as women?'

Oli stayed deadpan.

'Go look it up on your smartphone. If you don't know what I'm talking about, you should get out more.'

The heckler's mates ruffled his hair.

'I see the demand for gay rights as part of a wider fight for equality.' He glanced at Simon. 'You can't just dismiss it as political correctness gone mad.'

The next question was also directed at Oli.

'Are people born gay?'

'Beats me,' Oli replied.

His answer got a few shouts of disbelief.

'No, that's not a cop-out. Most gay people say they feel different even before they're interested in sex. I know I did. Are we born that way? I'm no expert.'

Mr Hudson leaned forward.

'Another question, please.'

'This is for both candidates,' said a girl sitting three seats away. 'Have you ever kissed a boy?'

'I think that's a bit personal,' said Mr Hudson. 'We're discussing political correctness. You don't have to answer, candidates.'

Simon scowled.

'No.'

Oli waited a beat then a smile came over his face.

'No need to be coy about it. Yes.'

Connor was on his second warning, but Jake wasn't.

'Aren't you ashamed of yourself?' he said. 'The thought of two boys going at it makes me sick.'

Mr Hudson went to interrupt him, but Oli caught his eye.

'That's all right, Sir. I'll answer him.'

He cleared his throat.

'Did you know, Jake,' he said, 'that research by US psychologists claims 80 per cent of men who are anti-gay have secret homosexual feelings themselves?'

Jake's face drained of blood. He searched in vain for a comeback before slumping in his chair. Oli shifted his gaze pointedly from Jake to Connor. Peals of laughter engulfed the hall. The applause turned into a standing ovation from three-quarters of the audience. Two boys tousled Connor's hair and he tried to elbow them away. Mr Hudson finally calmed the audience down and the candidates made their closing remarks. We crowded round Oli on the way out.

'I loved that crack at Jake and Connor,' Jess said. 'They will never live it down.'

'Ow, that's a bad dose of Sphenopalatine Ganglioneuralgia!'

Anthony swallowed his mouthful of ice cream and waited for Charlie to explain the torrent of gobbledegook. Charlie fancied himself, among other things, as an edgy and comic observer of twenty-first-century life, but came across as a geek with a bad dose of verbal diarrhoea.

'What are you on about now?'

'Ice cream brain-freeze, that headache you get when it gets stuck to the top of your mouth.'

'Is that what they call it, Spendodoodle Gangliowhatsit?'

'It is.'

'So what did you think about the debate?'

'Oli Hampshire dealt well with that heckler.'

'Didn't he just? Jake and Connor deflated like balloons.' Charlie finished the ice cream, dropped the stick in the bin and treated Anthony to a meaningful stare. 'That might have been a mistake.'

He held an invisible noose over his head, closed his eyes and stuck out his tongue.

'How's that?'

'You've obviously not spent much time round Martendale.'

'No, I don't really know the place. That's where you live, isn't it?'

'Yes, and nobody who has any dealings with Brian Hughes would dare to make fun of his family.'

'Bad news, is he?'

'I actually feel sorry for Connor. He's terrified of his old man. Brian Hughes is a few slates short of a roof. He got done for road rage a while back. He claimed this guy cut him up on a roundabout. He chased him for over a mile and dragged him out of the car at traffic lights. He battered the poor sod with a wheel brace. Did eighteen months for it.'

'I wonder if Oli knew any of that when he used that put-down.'

'I don't think so. Oli should follow my example and steer well clear. Taking risks is against my religion. I'm a devout coward. What about you?'

The question crept under Anthony's guard.

'Oh, I'm a coward.' He had the night in Cartmel Park in his head. He struck his leg with his fist. 'I hate myself for it.'

Charlie was thrown by Anthony's reaction.

'Are we having the same conversation here? I was only joking.'

Anthony recovered quickly.

'Yes, me too.'

'You've got a weird sense of humour, mate. I don't get it. One minute you're here on Planet Normal, then you're off in some whole other galaxy.'

It was time for Anthony to reroute the conversation.

'I looked up that song you were humming yesterday.'

'*We Are Young*?'

'Yes, there's an acoustic version, guitar, piano, voice. It shouldn't be a problem.'

He played the YouTube clip on his Android.

'I think that's my song. The guitar is simple. Tough on the voice, but I think I can do it. What do you think?'

'Love it.'

Anthony smiled. He hadn't felt this happy since before his mother met Mosley.

I'M THE 0.9 CHILD

Sunday, 9 March 2014

The weather was good enough to get the bike out. Dad preferred the car when it was wet. He had always been protective, over-protective Rosie used to say. She had a point. We spent the day in the North Lakes. On the way back we pulled into Tebay services, stowed our helmets in the top box and went inside.

'Cake?'

I smiled.

'Are you kidding? Of course, cake.'

He went for a slab of chocolate cake. I chose a scone the size of a boulder.

'Did Mum tell you they've fixed the date for the trial?'

His eyes, usually so soft, went hard, like stones.

'When did she hear?'

'Not sure. She told me yesterday, but I think she's been hanging on to the letter for a while. All this stuff with Anthony Broad, I don't think she wanted to spring anything else on me.'

'How are you coping with that? I suppose you see him all the time.'

'I do my best to ignore him.'

That wasn't the right word. Ignore is something active. I looked away on purpose. I evaded him. Most of the time,

I faded away at his approach, the ghost girl. Even if Mum hadn't told me to steer clear, would I have confronted him? I don't know.

'I don't suppose there's any alternative. Maybe that boy is as much of a victim as we are.'

I felt a buzz of shock.

'You don't mean that!'

'Would I have been any different if I'd been one of those onlookers? I like to think I'd have come forward as a witness, but I'm not sure.' He sipped his tea. 'Did I ever tell you about a lad called Eddie Morris?'

'I don't think so.'

'He was a year older than me. I was in top juniors, Year 6 these days. He was at secondary school. I was out with my mate, Danny. We saw him in the distance and started shouting insults.'

'Why?'

'God knows. Anyway, we thought he'd gone, then there he was right behind us on his bike. He'd circled round the back somehow. Danny legged it. Well, Eddie gets off his bike and gives me a clip round the ear. He says I'm his prisoner. He makes me run alongside him. I'm bricking it. I'd do whatever he says. He kept me a kind of prisoner for two hours, humiliating me. I was ashamed of myself for days after.'

'Why didn't you run like Danny?'

'I was scared. Pathetic really. Eddie wasn't much bigger than me, but I just gave in and made myself his slave. People are always ready to tell you about the brave things they've done. They hide the stuff they don't want to admit.' He finished his cake. 'Maybe I kind of understand this Anthony lad.'

That was a step too far.

'He watched while they killed our Rosie!'

The people on the next table stared. I dropped my eyes.

'Sorry, Dad.'

'Don't be. Maybe I'm the one who should say sorry. I'm beat, love, broken. I'm not like your mum. I can't handle this.'

'But you're going to the trial, aren't you? She needs you there.'

'I don't know.'

'Oh, Dad.'

'Don't judge me, Eve. They took my little girl. Twenty years of love we put into Rosie. I . . .' He lost control for a second. 'I held her in my arms when she was born. I was made to be a dad. I loved everything about it.' He laughed. 'I even started to act responsibly, imagine that, Jack-the-Lad becomes Dave the Dad.'

I had never heard him talk like this.

'Rosie was my little doll. She was into everything, so curious and intense about things. She had her own mind, that one. Did we ever tell you about her sleeping in a drawer?'

I had heard the story over and over again, but I let him tell it as if it was the first time.

'You'll be too young to remember. She decided she didn't want to sleep in a bed. For a while she made a kind of nest out of one of the big drawers where you store bedding.'

'I wonder why she wanted to do that.'

'With our Rosie you didn't ask questions like that. She was a contrary little madam. She made her own rules.'

I nodded. In the family mythology Rosie was their dark goddess. I was just a mortal.

'And those bastards took her away. For what? For kicks? For fun?'

I chose the moment to make my point.

'That's why you should be with Mum at the trial, to see them sent down.'

'The court will make its decision whether I'm there or not. I won't make any difference. And no matter what Cathy thinks, neither will she. The law will do its thing. We will get our morsel of justice, but it won't be enough. What's the return on a stolen life?'

I thought of Mum back home.

'She needs you, Dad. You think she's strong, but she's struggling. Don't do this.'

He blew out his cheeks.

'I can't be there. Nothing that happened makes any sense. I can't face it, Eve. Nobody cares what happens to the victims' families anyway. They don't want our story.'

I wanted to say something, but I wasn't the one who spoke next. I had been aware of the elderly couple next to us for some time. They were listening to our conversation. In the silence that followed Dad's howl of pain, they leaned across.

'Excuse me, I hope you don't think we're being nosy or intrusive.'

Dad stared, confused.

'My name is Derek Johnson. This is my wife, Trish. We . . .' He glanced at his wife. 'We know who you are. We read about what happened. We wanted to say that our thoughts are with you. We've got a daughter ourselves. We can't imagine what you're going through.'

They got up to go. Mr Johnson held out his hand

and Dad shook it. He barely seemed aware what was happening.

'Good luck, mate. Just don't despair, all right. Those animals, they don't represent this country.'

With that, they went.

'See, Dad,' I said, 'there are good people in the world.'

Dad watched them all the way to the car.

'I know, love, but it takes a hell of a lot of people to do good. It only takes one or two to do evil.'

The row started within minutes of us getting back. I couldn't listen to them quarrelling. I fled upstairs, slammed the door shut and curled up in my window seat, screwing clenched fists into my eyes. In the end, the argument spilled into the hall.

'Don't you understand, Cath? It's taking over your life. It's becoming an obsession.'

'How dare you!'

He said something I couldn't make out.

'Rosie was my child, Dave. If I can't fight for her, what kind of mother am I?'

'You've got to come to terms with it. It's eating away at you. She isn't coming back.'

Mum turned on him.

'She filled our world once. She can't just vanish because her heart stopped beating.'

'She's gone. End of. There's nothing left but memories.'

I saw my family fading. One day we would all be gone.

'She isn't gone,' Mum said. 'For as long as I live and breathe, she will be here in my head. I can't close my eyes without seeing her. That little girl occupied a place in the universe. There is a hole where she once walked this Earth.'

'I don't even understand what you're saying.'

'I am saying that I have got to fill that hole. I have got to put her back in the world. I will fight for justice with every fibre of my being. That's how she will go on. We are setting up a campaign in her name . . .'

'I read the papers, Cath. I know what you're doing.'

He was referring to the all-day gig they held at the football ground. Eight bands played that day, free of charge.

'Then join us. People ask me why you don't come to the meetings.'

'Don't try to make out that I loved her less. She was everything to me.'

Mum's voice softened.

'I would never accuse you of that. I wish you could join me, that's all. People ask where you are.'

'And what do you say?'

'I tell them you've got your own way of grieving. But hear me out, Dave. The only way we can make sense of this is to do something to make sure no other kids die like she did.'

'Still think you can change the world, eh?'

'I've got to think that.'

He had the door open.

'Well, I don't know any more. Don't get me wrong. I haven't changed my views. I just don't have the same faith in people any more.'

'I refuse to stop fighting.'

'Fine, that's your choice. You find your way of getting through the day. I'll find mine. I'm going.' He paused to shout upstairs. 'See you, Eve love.'

I forced out a reply.

'See you, Dad.'

The bike roared as he rode away.

M um sensed my presence behind her.
'I'm sorry you had to hear that.'

I changed the subject. Her computer was on and I could see Rosie's face on the new campaign website. The impish smile belied the horrific story it told.

'Is that what it's going to look like?'

'It's one design.' She clicked the mouse. 'This is another. What do you think?'

'The red and black background. It's what Rosie would have chosen. When will it be ready?'

'The designer says we're close. I'm going to be doing a lot of meetings, going into schools, telling Rosie's story. You're going to have to fend for yourself a bit. Are you OK with that?'

'With you all the way, Mum.'

She leaned her head against me. Maybe she didn't hear the weariness in my voice. Maybe she didn't want to.

'I wish your dad was.'

'He's with you too, in his own way.'

She kept her head against my shoulder.

'You're very wise, Eve.'

This was madness. She heard wisdom, strength and all the while I heard the echoes of my own weakness. I was crumbling inside. This time I was unable to hide my misery.

'No, I'm not!'

The words came flying out like shards of glass.

'Hey, what is this?'

'Rosie was the wise one. She knew about ecology and

renewables and peace and why wars are wrong and why they do animal experiments and why parliament doesn't listen to the people. She knew why the banks crashed and why poor people pay for the mistakes of the rich. She knew why people starve when the world can grow more food than it needs . . .'

I ran out of breath and stood there trembling.

'Eve?'

'I'm sorry. I'm not good enough. I can't live up to her memory. I'm the 0.9 child. She was about other people and I'm only about me. I'm the selfish one, the runt. Mum, I've always been second best. Maybe it should have been me that night, not her.'

She was out of her seat with her arms round me. Her fingers were in my hair and her tears were on my face.

'I can't even tell Anthony what I think of him. She was brave and I'm not. She was everything and I'm . . .' I talked through the sobs. 'I am nothing.'

'Eve, oh, I'm sorry, Evie. I didn't think. I've been so wrapped up in the court case and the campaign. How long have you been feeling this way?'

I shook my head. I couldn't answer.

Her fingertips stroked my cheeks. 'You were so different, the pair of you. Maybe she commanded attention in a way you didn't. But you're my thoughtful, beautiful girl. Your dad and I love you to bits. We've never compared the two of you. Love isn't like that. If I let you feel anything less than my precious child, I'm so sorry.'

She let me slip out of her embrace and I stumbled to the settee. She was immediately by my side.

'It's so hard,' I told her. 'When Anthony appeared that day, when I heard Mrs Rawmarsh say his name . . .'

Then I let her hold me. Neither of us spoke another word.

YOU'RE GOING TO REMEMBER ME

Tuesday, 11 March 2014

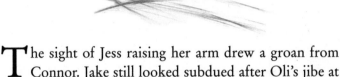

The sight of Jess raising her arm drew a groan from Connor. Jake still looked subdued after Oli's jibe at the hustings. He'd taken a lot of stick. I had been wary of the pair ever since I heard the stories about Connor's dad.

'You have a question, Jess?'

'Yes, we voted on the debate yesterday afternoon. When do we get the result?'

'You'll know tomorrow. OK, there is one more announcement. On Thursday evening it is the final of *Shackleton's Got Talent*, starting at seven o'clock. Entrance is strictly by ticket only. At the last count we had fifty-five tickets left. It is first come, first served. Right, off you go to your classes.'

Connor barged Jess out of the way as we left the room, making her stumble into me. I caught my hip on a desk and winced at the pain.

'Hey you,' Jess snapped. 'Aren't you going to apologise?'

Connor sneered.

'In your dreams.'

I wanted to drag her away, but she was trembling with fury.

'Just because Oli showed you up in front of everybody.'

'He showed himself up, the poof.'

'You're pathetic. Oli ran rings round you.'

'That mouth of his is going to get him in trouble.'

My flesh crawled. Jess spat out her frustration.

'You're a pig, Connor.'

'And you're a bitch.'

I was trying to get Jess away. She was twisting round, glaring. Connor laughed in her face.

'You need to watch Connor,' I told her.

'Yes, you already said.'

'Jess, please take me seriously. I keep hearing more stuff about that family. His dad is really dangerous.'

Jess was stubborn.

'Oli isn't scared of anybody.'

I made a grab for her hand.

'Listen to me. This is no time for grand gestures. More than anyone, I know what people like that can do. Maybe Oli should be worried. Please tell him to be careful.'

I gave her hand a squeeze. She squeezed back.

'It's OK, worrywart, nothing's going to happen.'

'Jess, please. I'm begging you. Talk to Oli.'

'Connor Hughes is just a sad, sorry moron. He doesn't bother me. Forget him.'

Connor was turning the corner. He seemed to have overheard at least part of the conversation. He pointed a finger at Jess.

'Oh, you're going to remember me, bitch, you and your stinking perv of a brother.'

Mrs Rawmarsh had missed the first part of the incident. Halfway down the corridor, she stopped and spun round.

'Connor, that's enough!'

He sauntered off with Jake following in his wake. Jess looked shaken.

'Did you hear what he called me, Miss? And what he said about Oli?'

'I'll be having a word with Mr Hudson, Jess. I'm afraid the debate has stirred up some ugly feelings. We're keeping our eye on Connor.'

But they weren't, not really.

We were on our way into the dining hall when Rehana drew Jess's attention to the posters advertising the Great Debate. Simon's photograph was untouched. Oli's was covered with insults scrawled in felt tip: poof, queer, bum boy. There were also a series of crudely scribbled, obscene drawings. Jess tore the posters down. With the posters still in her fists she marched towards the serving hatch.

'What are you doing?' I hissed as I made a grab for her. She sailed out of my grasp.

'I'm going to make people see sense.'

She barged her way to the front of the queue, ignoring the angry protests that bubbled around her. She looked around for a moment then snatched a ladle and pounded it on the metal counter. Heads turned. A hush fell over the usually noisy diners.

'Looks like I've got your attention,' Jess announced in a clear, strong voice. 'This won't take long.'

One of the lunchtime assistants was hurrying her way, but Jess was in full flow.

'Some of you might have seen these. Somebody . . .' Her gaze travelled around the room. 'Somebody who hasn't got the guts to say anything to my brother's face has scrawled insults all over his picture. Anyone want to own up?

'Oh, come on, somebody here knows who did it. Don't be shy. If you've got something to say, come out with it.'

The silence continued. She spotted Jake and Connor skulking in a corner.

'Anyone?' She waited a beat. 'I'll give you another

chance. You were quick enough to write this filth. I want whoever did it to come up here and say why.'

She waited. I could see her trembling.

'Fine, that's typical of the kind of scumbag who uses words like this. That's what bigots are like. They hide in the dark. Do you want to hear what it says?'

Still, no one spoke. The lunchtime assistant just stood there.

'Well, I'm going to read it anyway. You can laugh if you like, that's what people do when you use words like this. But when you're done laughing I want you to think about them and the harm they can do. Imagine what it's like if you hear them all the time, if people don't respect you for who you are.' She flattened the posters on the counter and read each word, jabbing at them with her finger. 'Poof, queer, bum boy. Oh, there's one I missed, perv. Hey, the idiot who wrote this spelled it right.' She clapped her hands sarcastically. 'Four whole letters, three consonants and a vowel. Well done!'

She glared at her audience, eyes flashing with indignation.

'Do you find them funny? Good, because I'd come over there and wipe the stupid, ignorant grin off your faces. Oli, my beautiful brother . . . is . . . gay. Get it? But he is so much more than that. He is the best brother anybody could have. He is kind, caring and considerate. He listens to my problems when I'm down. More than that, he is so brave. It can't be easy to stand up in front of the whole school and come out, but that's what he did. I love him and I am so proud of him. Anybody wants to hurt my brother, they are going to have to come through me. Got that?'

There wasn't a sound. Then, without any warning, Jess ran out of the room. She left a shoe behind. I scooped it up and pursued her into the yard. Behind me there was a round of applause that lasted long after I had chased her down to a quiet corner by the library. She was clawing tears from her eyes.

'Aw, Eve, what have I done now?'

It took her three goes to get her foot in the shoe.

'You told the truth.'

'Oh God, I've made a complete idiot of myself in front of the whole school.'

'Jess, they loved you.'

My arm slid round her shoulder. We didn't say much, just clung to each other. That's when I became aware of a pair of figures looming over us. Jess stood up to face Mrs Rawmarsh and Mr Hudson.

'I'm in trouble, aren't I?'

'Actually, no, you're not.'

Jess was confused.

'I threw one hell of a hissy fit in the dining hall.'

Mr Hudson smiled.

'You just made a very passionate, eloquent speech. You stuck up for equal rights.'

'Did I? I thought I was backing Oli.'

'The bit I heard went a bit further than a defence of your brother.'

Mrs Rawmarsh took her cue from him.

'You might have been a little more diplomatic about how you did it, but you have nothing to worry about, Jess.' She smiled. 'Far from it. We're not going to tell the rest of the school until tomorrow, but Oli won the debate by a landslide.'

I knew the moment I slid into the passenger seat that something was wrong.

'Mum?'

She didn't respond, but I saw the way she was gripping the steering wheel.

'What's happened?'

She pulled away. When I finally got an answer her voice was thick with emotion.

'I went round to see Emma Broad.'

The news struck me like a punch in the stomach.

'This is bad news, isn't it?'

'I waited outside the flat until Anthony arrived home from school. You should have seen the look on his face when he saw me. He froze. I never saw myself as somebody to be feared. I told him I knew his mother was in the flat.'

She took a left onto the Manchester Road. For a moment she stopped speaking. Streetlamps stuttered in the dark. She picked up the story.

'She must have seen us from the window. Next moment the door flew open and she started to drag him inside. She wasn't in any mood to listen. She told me to leave her son alone. She was screaming.'

'Oh Mum, I was worried something like this was going to happen.'

'Your dad warned me. I wanted a jury to hear what those thugs did to my little girl. The truth has got to come out.'

She parked in front of the house, her front tyre scuffing the kerb.

'She said I was a mad woman. She said . . .' Her eyes were desperate. 'She accused me of stalking her son. I didn't get a chance to explain myself.'

I hated seeing her like this. I hated the misery that was choking her. She had ridden rapids of despair in the past year. It was as if she was being made to go through Rosie's death over and over again. There was no peace, no closure.

'Eve, I needed to make her understand. I told her I had lost a child. I appealed to her as a mother.' Her chin quivered. 'She wouldn't listen to a word I said. All she could see was a woman who was putting her son in danger.' She started to sob. 'She threatened to call the police. After everything I've been through, she was going to call the police on *me*.'

'Oh, Mum!'

I did my best to comfort her, but I had to sit beside her while the past continued to torture her. That's when I remembered the way Jess had stood in front of the whole school and testified for Oli. Suddenly I knew what I had to do. From that moment I started to plan.

HAVING A PARTY?

Wednesday, 12 March 2014

Mr Hudson announced the winner of the Great Debate at morning assembly. Anthony barely registered a word. Jess was two rows ahead and three seats to his left. She led the applause for Oli, her whole body shaking as she clapped her hands. Anthony watched the way her ponytail bobbed up and down.

Why couldn't things be different? She was everything he wanted in a girl. She was bubbly, friendly, intelligent, attractive. He imagined the scent of her hair, wondered what it would be like to spend a whole evening with her, talking about all kinds of dreams and nonsense. That would have been possible but for what happened in Cartmel Park on a hot, savage night in August.

A twist of fate meant they could never be together. Eve's mother had seen to that. He couldn't believe she had come round again, pursuing him, pushing him into Mosley's path. What if he found them? Him and Mum? What if it all started again? Eve's mother was never going to let it go. The feelings she stirred in him went beyond fear. Shame, guilt, humiliation all came shrieking out of the past to haunt him. She could not even be hated. She could not be scrubbed from his conscience. Her cause was too just.

Mr Hudson closed the assembly and people started to file out, form by form. Jess was in front. It took Anthony a moment to force himself to touch her arm as she went to follow Eve outside. The shudder when she realised whose hand it was, the blaze of contempt in her eyes, told him she knew all about Cartmel Park.

'Jess, can I talk to you?'

Her face was a mask, her features set against him, hard, cold, unresponsive.

'You've got a nerve! I know what you did. I know all about you.'

There were a few glances from the passing students, but few showed any particular curiosity.

'Oh, don't worry,' she continued. 'I'm not going to make a scene. The school wants this thing kept quiet. Eve has her reasons too. Fine, I'm not going to rock the boat. But don't come near me ever again.'

'Jess . . .'

He was aware of Eve watching him. She had her mother's eyes. It wasn't just the colour. It was the quality of accusation in them.

'I don't want to hear it, Anthony. First you stand by while those animals attack Rosie. Then you follow Eve here . . .'

He couldn't let it pass without protest.

'It wasn't like that! If I'd known, I would never have let Mum choose this school.'

'Finally,' Jess continued, dismissing his objections, 'you let me make a fool of myself.' She dropped her voice to an outraged whisper. 'You don't say a thing even though you know what it must be doing to my best friend to see us together.'

He wanted to explain. If only he could make her see that the picture she had of him was false.

'What kind of person does that, Anthony? I'm going now. Don't you dare follow me or I'll scream the place down.' She jabbed a finger in his direction. 'And I know you wouldn't want to attract any more attention to yourself.'

He watched her go. Every word had drawn blood.

Mrs Rawmarsh looked up when she heard the knock.

'Come in.'

She saw who it was and closed the lid of her laptop.

'Has something happened? Is this about Eve Morrison?'

'In a way. It's about Jess.'

He had her attention.

'Go on.'

'Eve's told her. We ... we kind of had words.'

'Oh, Anthony.' She thought for a moment. 'Did many people overhear this conversation?'

'I saw a few people look our way, but I don't think they stopped to listen.' A pause. 'No, I don't think that's a worry.'

'So what do you want, Anthony?'

'I can't do the song tomorrow.'

'I beg your pardon?'

'It doesn't seem right. I mean, I don't deserve to be there.'

She told him to sit down.

'You're a talented lad, Anthony ...'

He interrupted her.

'I can't sing in front of all those people. I'm ashamed of what I did ... what I didn't do.'

'Mr McKechnie spoke to your mother at length,

Anthony. We all understand what happened. You were in the wrong place at the wrong time, that's all.' He knew that wasn't even remotely true. She hadn't been there.

'I don't know. What if Eve comes?'

Mrs Rawmarsh turned to her laptop.

'I can soon check. I've got the list of ticket sales. Let's see. OK, Jessica and Oli are here. They are coming with their parents.'

He cleared his throat.

'What about Eve?'

Mrs Rawmarsh checked twice.

'No, Eve isn't coming. Anthony, you've got a great choice of song and you perform it well. Don't drop it on a whim.' She leaned forward. 'This might be just the thing to help you finally settle in at Shackleton. You want that, don't you?'

Of course that's what he wanted. He could barely imagine what that would feel like. He'd been walking on a road of shame and the tar stuck to his shoes.

'Yes, but Jess is going to be there in the audience, staring at me, knowing what I did.'

'You can't keep running all your life, Anthony.'

He failed to meet her gaze. Finally, he nodded.

'OK, I'll play.'

I wanted to do it then. I wanted to bring the school to a halt, march into the middle of the yard and demand everybody's attention. I wanted to draw their eyes to me, just as Jess had done when she silenced the dining hall. She stood up for her living brother, but here I was letting Anthony spit on my sister's grave.

He had to understand the pain that drove Mum to his door. Did he know shame? Did he have a conscience? I held myself in check. What was the point of anger, of emotion? I would only shout and scream and crumple into helpless tears. My weakness would be his strength. I imagined how I would stumble through a sobbing, incoherent tirade that nobody heard or understood. I didn't have Jess's composure.

I had to find another way, one that would allow me to walk tall. I had to summon a ghost and stand inside her translucent presence. I had to be an avenging Fury exposing the wrongdoer.

I went as far as the Wizard's Lair, moving fast, feeling my shoes thud on the pavement. All those days I shrank from responsibility. Now I was purposeful, my rage shaped and fashioned into a weapon, a tool of revenge and testament.

One section of the shop hired out fancy dress, mostly of the macabre variety: zombies, vampires, demons. There was a back room that stocked vinyl records and CDs. I knew some of the bands but not all. There were albums by The Velvet Underground, Buffalo Springfield, Jefferson Airplane, Deep Purple, Country Joe and the

Fish, Lindisfarne, Wishbone Ash and Cream, among others. There were artists like Gil Scott-Heron, Joan Baez, Bob Dylan, Jimi Hendrix, Janis Joplin and Melanie Safka, names that would mean absolutely nothing to Rehana and Hannah. I wasn't interested in the fancy dress or the shelves of retro music. None of it meant a thing to me. It was the third section of the shop that I had come to explore. It specialised in theatrical make-up and prosthetics, grotesque noses, fake scabs and scars, green, warty noses and goblin ears. I finally found what I was looking for and paid for the small, plastic bottle.

'Having a party?' the guy behind the counter asked.

'Mm,' I answered, 'something like that.'

The timing worked out perfectly. Mum had a meeting in Preston.

'We can get leaflets and videos done professionally,' she said in the brief few minutes we had together before she rushed to the car and sped towards the motorway.

The idea was that speakers were going to go into schools and tackle prejudice. This sort of thing happened all the time. I'd lost track of the number of newspaper and TV interviews she had done. No way could I ever be like her, but I could do something. I *was* going to do something. Anthony would never forget that he had stood by while Rosie was destroyed.

I thought of my brave mum standing in the street pleading with him and his monster of a mother. All this time I had been numb. I had never once offered to accompany Mum to a meeting, to address envelopes or attend a fundraising gig. The more she threw herself into organising the campaign, the more I shrank.

I wasn't going to sit still any more. I opened the door to Rosie's room. Her stuff was everywhere. I opened the wardrobe doors and sat on the edge of the bed. I was taller than Rosie. I would have to choose the right set of clothes. The image had to be perfect. It had to burn itself into the minds of my audience.

I was patient. I tried on the skirts, examined myself in the mirror. I narrowed the choice down to two. Now I had to find a matching blouse. That was harder. Finally, I found one that fitted. It looked sleek and dark, exactly what I wanted. I found the lacy, fingerless gloves she liked.

I zipped up the skirt and buttoned the leather boots. I looked at my reflection.

That's when I discovered my biggest problem. How could I slip into the skin of my sister with my long, straight hair? What could I do that would remotely compare with her mass of black and scarlet dreads? I started tugging at drawers, frantically rummaging through her belongings.

I glanced at my phone. I was running out of time. Then there it was. Of course. How could I have forgotten? We did this amazing road trip through France and Spain a few summers back. One day, in a small town in Andalucia, Rosie squealed with delight. There was a stall selling mantillas, the light veils that traditionally covered a woman's head and shoulders. She put together a collection over the years, some white, mostly black. I scraped back my hair so severely it was painful. When I peered at my reflection wearing the mantilla, the transformation was complete. I spent a few minutes making up my face and smiled.

I was ready.

The spotlight picked out Mrs Rawmarsh.

'Your votes have been counted, ladies and gentlemen. Behind me are all our talented entrants.'

There was some shuffling of feet.

'In a moment I will announce the three finalists. They will perform again then there will be a ten-minute intermission while you vote for the very last time. After that we will have the winner of *Shackleton's Got Talent*.'

She gave her broadest smile.

'In no particular order,' Mrs Rawmarsh began, 'our first finalist is ...'

She beamed through the long pause.

'... comedian Shaun Carrick. I am sure Mr Hudson enjoyed the Godfather joke. Our second finalist is ...'

She took even longer over this announcement.

'... yes, it's Isobel Hammill.'

'Our third and last finalist is ...'

Anthony held a fixed expression. He was determined not to show any pleasure or disappointment.

'... guitarist and singer Anthony Broad.'

The strength of the audience's reaction made him favourite to win. The contestants who had not made it to the final left the stage to applause.

'OK,' Mrs Rawmarsh said, 'let's hear it for our fabulous finalists.'

When the applause died down, Anthony and Isobel left the stage.

'You're going to win,' Isobel said. 'You can tell by the response.'

'You're really good too, you know.'

Isobel laughed. 'And you're a gentleman.'

Anthony edged along the curtain and searched for Jess. She was in the third row with Oli and her parents. He fought to control his nerves. His mother was there somewhere. It was only now that he realised he wanted to win for her. Life had been kicking her around for so long, she refused to believe it would ever get better. They still lived in constant fear of Mosley. It was time she had something to smile about, even if it was something as stupid as a school talent show. Shaun gave him a nudge.

'They called your name, Anthony. Wake up.'

He passed Isobel as she made her way off stage.

'Break a leg,' she whispered.

He perched on a stool. Mrs Rawmarsh was opposite him, her fingers hovering over the piano. He took a deep breath and used his plectrum to tap out the intro on the body of the guitar. Mrs Rawmarsh came in after a few seconds and he started to sing. It was good to perform in public again. He had missed the band. He didn't look at the audience. He wrapped himself in the song, eyes closed as he hit the top notes. He raised his hand to stop the piano accompaniment and finished it a cappella. There was a moment's silence then applause engulfed him. As he left the stage Isobel gave him a hug.

'You smashed it, Ant. Nice touch at the end.'

He frowned.

'Nobody's ever called me Ant in my life.'

She smiled.

'There's a first time for everything.'

It took him a few moments to locate his mother in the crowd around the refreshments. People were putting their voting slips in the ballot boxes to the left and right of the catering tables.

'That was the best yet,' she said. 'You've got to win.'

He noticed a couple of sixth formers collecting the ballot boxes and taking them over to a trestle table to be counted.

'You would say that. You're my mum.'

He was aware of Jess over to his left, watching him. She seemed curious about his mother. Was it possible, even now, that she would make some kind of scene? He felt his stomach knot. Somebody flicked the light switches a couple of times.

'Ladies and gentlemen,' Mrs Rawmarsh announced. 'Please take your seats. We are ready to announce tonight's winner.'

Just a few more minutes, he thought. Please Jess, he prayed silently, don't say anything. I never wanted anyone to get hurt. When they took Rosie's life, they took mine too. Let me have this moment.

I walked down the Manchester Road, surrounded by the kind of deep, quiet blackness that wraps you in its folds. The moon flitted in and out of the clouds, glimmering briefly before sinking back into the heavy gloom. Soon, I followed the line of bleary lights up the hill towards the school. There was a shout from a passing car.

'Mosher. Weirdo-o-o-o.'

There was a burst of laughter before it was lost in the hiss of traffic. I almost turned back at that. This was the flaw in my plan. I had thought through everything except the long walk across town. How did Rosie do this every day? I felt so self-conscious and vulnerable. I had climbed into her skin in more ways than one.

I wasn't easy with what I had to do. Once I was in the school grounds I slipped past. There was nobody in the school foyer. I breathed a sigh of relief and edged towards the hall. I could hear a female voice. Peering inside, I recognised Isobel. Then there he was, up next, Anthony. His voice was clear, his singing controlled. I froze for a moment. That song . . . He was good. I pressed my fingernails into my thigh, pinching away any possibility of sympathy.

I would not be a frightened, anxious sixteen-year-old. I would be an avenging angel, taking wing on behalf of my murdered sister, my tortured mother. I felt the bottle in my hand. The timing had to be right.

Anthony finished to thunderous applause. They liked him. I felt every whoop of appreciation as a barb, an insult to Rosie's memory, a slap in my mother's face. Mrs Rawmarsh was on stage, holding the golden envelope in her hands. Here it was, the announcement. There was no longer any doubt. He was going to win. I had planned for this moment, rehearsed the timing. I would let him have his moment of glory. Let him gloat. Let him think there would be no consequences for his actions. Let him believe.

'The winner of *Shackleton's Got Talent*,' Mrs Rawmarsh announced, 'is . . .'

The drumroll of stamping feet followed. Jess looked away, disgusted. That's when she saw the figure gliding towards the stage, the gash of scarlet that ran from black lips onto ashen skin. Other people had seen her too. There was an undercurrent of murmurs rippling through the expectant silence.

'That's Eve!'

'The winner,' Mrs Rawmarsh repeated, building the tension, 'is . . .'

She was oblivious to the dark ghost closing on Anthony. Eve had reached the steps at the side of the stage. Mr Hudson at last noticed her and stumbled forward, making a grab for Eve's sleeve.

'. . . Anthony Broad.'

The wave of cheering and applause swept away the voices of concern.

'Anthony's prize is a gift voucher for £100. Let's hear it one more time for our amazing singer and guitarist. Anthony Broad.'

Jess was scrambling to her feet.

'I know what she's going to do!'

I don't know how I reached the stage. I didn't see the audience. I felt the bottle in my hand. I squeezed off the stopper and dipped a finger inside before running it along my lips, freshening the smear I had already applied. I felt a hand on my arm and shrugged it away. Somewhere in among the darkened rows of faces my name was called.

'Eve!'

Anthony registered my presence. He had a smile on his face and a gleam of pride in his eyes. His life was ahead of him. He would know other triumphs. Rosie would know none. She would fade until people struggled even to remember her name.

Once he saw me, the glow of victory drained from his face. There was the thunder of footsteps on the wooden stage. Voices around me. Nothing could stop me now.

I heard him beg.

'Don't. Eve, don't.'

But I saw my sister. I saw that pale, perfect, upraised face. I saw her and love guided my hand.

Eve's arm swung from left to right and sprayed a slash across Anthony's white T-shirt. In spite of Mr Hudson's best efforts she twisted, the red, gluey liquid spattering his face and shoulders right to left so that there was a bloody cross marking him. Jess heard the cries of dismay rising around her. She raced towards the stage. Already, Mr Hudson and Mrs Rawmarsh were guiding a sobbing Eve away. They succeeded in escorting her to a classroom across the corridor.

'Please let me in,' Jess pleaded. 'She will listen to me.'

'Stay with them,' Mrs Rawmarsh said. 'I'll check on Anthony.'

Jess lifted Eve's face with her fingers.

'Oh, Evie, why didn't you say anything?'

'I had to do something. He had his moment. What about Rosie? When does she get hers?'

Mascara tracks cut through the white face-paint. The fake blood was drying, caking her lips, forming twin paths from the corners of her mouth.

'Are they laughing at me?'

'Eve, nobody's laughing.' Jess thought for a moment. 'Does your mum know where you are?'

A shake of the head. Eve held out her phone.

'Can you call her for me?'

Jess found Mum in the address book.

'Cath? Hi, it's Jess. No, Eve's OK. She's here with me. There's no need to worry. There's been a bit of an incident, but she's fine. Yes, honestly, she's safe.' She took a breath. 'It's hard to explain on the phone. Can you come home?'

She hung up and brushed Eve's hair from her face.

'What am I going to do with you, eh? Your mum is just leaving Preston. She's on her way.'

Mrs Rawmarsh returned with Mr McKechnie in tow.

'What kind of state is Anthony in?' Mr Hudson asked.

'He's a bit shaken. He wanted to know how Eve was.'

Eve stared.

'He did what?'

Mr McKechnie pulled up a chair.

'He said he understood what you did. He said he deserved it.'

Eve took a tissue from the box on the table and scrubbed at the fake blood that still smeared her lips.

'Will he come forward? Will he tell the police what he knows?'

Mr McKechnie shook his head.

'He didn't say anything else. Eve, I think that's for another day.'

Anthony was sitting on the settee, staring in the direction of the TV. He could hear his mother crashing the pans in the kitchen.

'Do you want anything, Anthony?'

'No.'

He felt her presence behind him even before her reflection appeared in the TV screen.

'That stupid girl ruined your big night. She turned it into a pantomime.'

Anthony replied without turning round.

'It was already a pantomime. Why the hell did I go along with it? She was the only honest person in the room.'

'What's that supposed to mean? She humiliated you in front of the whole school. It was pure malice. I should have known she was going to do something like this.'

Anthony finally twisted in his seat to look at her.

'Can you hear yourself? Do you remember who she is? Her sister was murdered.'

She sat beside him.

'I don't know why you aren't more angry.'

'I should never have entered. Something like this was always going to happen. I left that girl to die, Mum. It was always going to come back to haunt me.'

'Don't say that! You're letting guilt poison your mind. You weren't to know what was going to happen. You left the park before the violence started.'

But that wasn't what had happened.

That wasn't it at all.

A BROKEN BIRD

Saturday, 10 August 2013

A nthony heard the knock.
'That'll be Gollum,' he said.

He let Gollum in.

'So what are we going to do?' Gollum asked.

'Don't mind as long as we get out of here,' Anthony grunted.

He watched Roy's thick fingers rubbing his mother's back. That's the way it was. He owned her. Anthony burned with shame that he didn't tear the spade-like hand from his mother's body.

'Here's trouble,' Roy said, stifling a yawn.

'Hi, Roy,' Gollum said.

'Don't stay out too late,' Mum said.

Roy was out of his seat. The backs of his bare thighs made a sucking sound on the leather.

'Stop fussing. You're turning him into a right poof.'

He had Anthony in a head lock. Anthony flailed, trying to get Roy off him. The reek of sour sweat made him feel sick. The brief struggle was over in seconds.

'Take him out, Gollum,' he said. 'Show him the night life.'

Anthony's mother tried to protest.

'Roy . . .'

He snapped his finger in her face.

'Not another word! You hear me? He's going. It'll give us some quality time together.'

Anthony saw Roy make a grab for his mother and pull her onto the settee next to him.

Anthony's cheeks burned. He caught his mother's eye. There was a kind of wounded apology there. He followed Gollum out, stealing a glance back at the house where he had never felt at home. The last year everything that was solid, familiar, reliable had broken apart.

'Here,' Gollum said, tossing him a can of Bud. 'It'll put hairs on your chest.'

'Where was that?'

'In my jacket.'

'Where are we going?'

'Cartmel Park.'

They wandered through the empty streets. Now and then somebody would stagger out of a Chinese chippy with a tray of chow mein or slowly congealing sausage and chips. Mostly, they were on their own with only the passing cars to observe their progress. Anthony glanced at Gollum and remembered the day he got his nickname. He was short, scrawny and desperately pale. He had wispy dark hair that seemed to cluster in clumps on his scalp. His eyes were wide and prominent. No one ever called him by his real name, Nathan.

They reached the middle of the park. Silhouetted figures moved about in the crumbling bandstand. Others spilled across the surrounding lawns.

They didn't notice the group of lads at first. There were groups of kids everywhere, talking, laughing, messing around.

'Hear about the carrot with brain damage?' Gollum said. 'He's a vegetable.'

One of the boys heard him. That's how they came to be near him when it happened. The leader of the group introduced himself as Bradley. It was a name Anthony would have reason to remember. He wanted to go, but Gollum was already wandering across to them.

'You'll never be a comedian,' Bradley said. 'You want to know what I'm going to do? Here's my master plan. Get some money, a car, find myself a fit woman. . .'

'Loads of fit women,' Gollum interrupted. He seemed to like his new acquaintance. Anthony couldn't fathom why.

'Yes, loads of fit women. Get wasted, get laid, that's life.'

'You'll need plenty of cash then,' Gollum said.

'You want to know where the money's coming from? Anywhere I can get it.'

'He's going to sell his body at Martendale Market,' one of the others said.

Bradley pushed him in the chest, obviously the alpha male.

'Don't even joke about things like that,' he snapped. 'What's wrong with you?'

'It was only a joke. You're touchy tonight.'

That's how they spent the next hour, drinking, exchanging banter, swapping stories with the other aimless groups who drifted by, or stopped for a few minutes and sat talking on the grass. They seemed to have a problem with Anthony. His silence, the way he tried to shrink into the shadows, made them single him out. Every few minutes one of them would remember he was there and blow cigarette smoke in his face. That's how they passed the time, until they saw the freaks. The couple stopped by the group to ask for directions. That was their first mistake. Their second was choosing Bradley Gorman.

'Hey look,' he said, 'big mosher, little mosher.'

Anthony saw the girl's wary look travelling round the couple of dozen youths who had been drawn to the bandstand.

'Do you come to drink blood?' somebody asked.

The girl's slender fingers ran down her boyfriend's arm, trying to communicate a warning.

'Yes, very droll,' the boyfriend said, seemingly oblivious. 'The guy at the garage said there was a taxi rank across the park. Which path do we take?'

Bradley didn't like the answer. He pushed off the bench where he was sitting.

'You taking the piss?' he demanded.

'I beg your pardon?'

'You called me a troll.'

'No, I said droll.'

'What's that?'

'You know, funny.'

Bradley's expression darkened.

'Why am I funny?' he demanded. 'What, like weird?'

'Not what I meant, friend ...'

Anthony froze.

'Look who's talking about weird. What's your name, slasher boy?'

The boyfriend let the comment go. 'I'm Paul. This is Rosie.'

'Row Zee,' somebody said. 'Like the back of a baseball stadium.'

'Very good,' Paul said. 'You're sharp.'

'Are you patronising me? You think you're better than me.'

'No, I thought you were quick ...'

Tension rippled round the group.

'Paul,' Rosie said. 'Let's go.'

'Hey, she talks,' Bradley said. 'The little doll talks through her nasty, black lips. I thought she was one of those ventriloquist's dummies. Get her to say gottle o' geer.'

He made a grab for her. Instinctively, Paul blocked his way. By now, menace was crackling round the group. Everything Paul said was another scrap of flesh tossed to the wolf pack.

'Maybe the moshers want a gottle o' geer.'

Bradley tilted his can and let the contents trickle on Paul's boots. Paul took a step back.

'Does she want a gottle o' geer?' Bradley asked, approaching Rosie.

'Don't do that,' Paul protested as Rosie shrank away.

Bradley stiffened.

'Are you telling me what to do, mosher?'

Gollum stirred. He didn't like the way things were going.

'Listen,' Rosie said, 'we don't want any trouble. We want to know which way to this taxi rank.'

'You not from round here?' one of the boys asked.

In the darkness Anthony didn't know who was who.

'Course they're not from round here,' a shadowy figure said. 'We don't have goths in Brierley.'

'You're mistaken,' Paul said. 'We've been to a party.'

A slight twitch in his left eye said he had made a mistake, but he had Bradley's interest.

'Where?'

'Sorry?'

'Where's this goth colony in Brierley? Maybe we should drop in.'

The gang was crowding closer.

'Yes, I fancy a party.'

'Let's have the address,' he said. 'We're going to pay the Brierley goths a visit.'

'I'm sorry. No can do.'

Bradley's face twisted into an expression of uncontrollable rage.

'Don't tell my mate what he can and can't do! The address. Now!'

'Leave them alone,' Gollum said. He stretched out an arm. 'The taxi rank is over there. Take the right fork. When you get to the skateboard park, go left.'

Rosie smiled a thank you and set off along the path. Paul was about to follow her when Bradley blocked his way.

'Where are you going, freak?'

'The taxi rank. I told you.'

'I haven't finished with you yet. You're going to give me that address.'

'No,' Paul said, 'I'm not.'

That's when Bradley threw the first punch.

It was as if there was a veil between them. Anthony watched Paul go down. This gentle, easy-going guy hadn't expected Bradley's punch. At no point in the conversation had he fully grasped the coiled menace these teenagers represented. There was a moment when his face was startled and cruelly aware then he crumpled to the ground. Bradley was a predator. He saw weakness and went after it, lashing out with his foot as his prey fell. He stamped on Paul as he hit the cracked tarmac path. The boy next to him was kicking too. Together they pounded their victim like a piece of meat.

'No.'

The protests came from Rosie and Gollum. Anthony was silent as he stood beneath the trees. With each kick the events before him became more distant.

'What the hell are you doing, man?' Gollum yelled. 'There's no call for this.'

One attacker spun round. His finger was in Gollum's face.

'You keep your nose out.'

'He's had enough. Oh, Christ, Bradley, you've got to stop. Not the man's head. Are you crazy?'

The others were shouting.

'Yeah, bang the moshers.'

Anthony heard the kicks. He saw Rosie trying to claw her way past them as they laughed and pushed her back. He was beyond numb, completely paralysed by the sudden explosion of violence. He could see everything, hear the whole thing, but he could no more have done what Gollum did, yelling for Bradley to stop, than he could have become weightless and flown. Gollum looked around desperately.

'Will somebody help me here?' His gaze fell on Anthony. 'You?'

When Anthony didn't move, he started to plead with some of the other onlookers. A girl detached herself from the crowd and called 999. Nobody else moved. Some were curious. Others grimaced or cried out, but they didn't intervene. Gollum threw himself at Bradley, tearing at his back.

'You mad bastard! You're going to kill him.'

'Bang the moshers! Smash the freaks!'

'Yes, have some, you slasher.'

That's when Rosie joined Paul on the ground. Anthony didn't see how it happened. He heard her cry then saw her black clothing flutter. She struggled into a kneeling position and cradled Paul's head on her lap.

'Please stop.'

Gollum echoed her words.

'Bradley, stop now. Just stop, man!'

Bradley did not stop. He cast Gollum aside like a piece of rag, drew back his foot and drove the dirty white trainer into Rosie's head. She lay like a broken bird, black wings folded on the ground. That's when Anthony ran. He pushed himself away from the wall of his own fear and ran. Voices followed him. Were they screams? Were they the sound of the pack egging Bradley on as he unleashed hell?

Tears burst from Anthony's eyes as he pounded through the gloom. The oaks formed a tunnel. The darkness sighed and simmered. Then he was on the main road, sobbing and gasping for breath, each lungful of air roaring in his chest like a storm. His only thought was that he had to escape. He ran out into the road. Tyres squealed. A man's voice yelled.

'Idiot!'

The car was gone, screaming off towards Brierley Top, the brooding hill that lowered in the distance. By the time he reached the estate he was walking, his breathing returning to normal. Only now, a mile from the crime, did he replay the events in his head. He could have yelled the way Gollum had. He could have joined him trying to pull him away. Later, as he fled from the park, he could have called 999 on his phone. That girl called the police. He'd done none of those things.

THE MARKING OF FLESH

Saturday, 10 August 2013

'Eve! Eve, wake up.'

Mum's voice wailed in the night. She ripped the door open. She was standing barefoot, her dressing gown clumsily knotted round her waist. Her hair was wild, her eyes wilder still.

'Rosie's been attacked.'

'Attacked? Attacked how?'

'She's in intensive care. Paul was with her.'

'Was he hurt too? I don't understand.'

'He's in a bad way. They've taken him to a different hospital. I'm in pieces here, love. I've been trying to get through to your dad at work. He's on nights and there's nobody on the switchboard.'

'What about his phone?'

'I keep getting his voicemail. It's a nightmare.'

Somehow she eventually got hold of him. He swung into the hospital car park moments after we arrived. We were by the main entrance when we heard him shout. He was hauling the bike up on its stand. They went in first, leaving me sitting on a red plastic chair in the corridor, still confused. Why would anybody attack Rosie? I heard a draught excluder purr and leapt up.

'How is she?' I asked.

'Eve, you've got to be strong. She's really swollen. I could hardly recognise her.'

A nurse led us into the ward. I don't even know how we got there. I don't remember going through any doors. I don't remember my footsteps. Rosie was such a mess. Her hair was in dreads the way she always wore it. Some of the locks had been torn from her scalp. She had two black eyes. There were marks on both arms and on her legs where they must have dragged her across the ground. Worst of all, there was a footprint in the bruising on her face. You could actually see the distinctive pattern of a training shoe sole.

'What did they do to her? How do you make a mark like that?'

Bewildered. That's the best description of how I felt. One minute I was lying in bed, warm, comfortable, half-awake, looking forward to going to the new dance class with Jess. Then I was trembling in the aftershock of an unspeakable wrong, staring at my beautiful sister lying unconscious in a hospital bed. Something occurred to me.

'Has she got her contacts in?'

Mum shook her head.

'No. I checked.'

So this was horror. The numbness, the ridiculous descent into the minutest of details, the grim routines of A&E. Mum's face was red and riven with tears, but it was Dad who upset me most. I couldn't remember ever seeing him cry before.

'Where's Paul?' I asked.

Mum told me the name of the hospital.

'Where's that?'

'Manchester.'

'Why aren't they in the same one?'

Her arms flopped at her side.

'He's supposed to be worse than Rosie,' she said. 'Touch and go, they say.'

'Oh, my God!'

I felt somebody's hand on my arm. It was the nurse, a woman in her thirties. She had a nose stud. Her eyes were dark and kind.

'Don't worry, your sister's going to be all right. We'll take good care of her.'

Behind her, a second nurse was dabbing at tears, contradicting her colleague's assurances.

'Mum, what happened?'

'All I know is they went to a party in Brierley, a couple of miles from their flat. They were attacked in Cartmel Park.'

'What were they doing there?'

'I don't know. I don't really know anything.'

Dad and I were in the hospital café. It was light and airy, with flowers on the table. It was an age before either of us spoke.

'She'll pull through,' Dad said. 'She's got to.'

'Mum's been gone a long time.'

'She'll be back soon.'

I couldn't get Rosie's face out of my mind.

'Why would anyone do something like that? Did you see the footprint?'

He squeezed his eyes tight shut.

'The attacker stamped on her face. I don't . . . What kind of person gets a twenty-year-old woman on the floor and jumps on her head?' He crushed his fists into his eyes. 'God almighty.' He puffed his cheeks, struggling with the emotions that were boiling out of him. 'Did you see her? Did you see Rosie's lovely face? It was like a football.'

He grabbed my hand.

'She went to a party. She wasn't late. She . . .'

He was trying to make sense of the senseless, to piece together something precious that had shattered into fragments.

'Don't, Dad,' I begged. 'I can't bear it.'

He found some kind of composure.

'I'm sorry, sorry.' His gaze flew round the room. 'I wonder how many people have sat here like this with their guts kicked out.'

Then Mum was with us, dropping into the seat next to me. Her hand ran over my shoulder and upper arm.

'Take Eve home, Dave. I'll stay.'

'No, Mum. I want to be here with you. With Rosie.'

'Seriously Eve, go home and get some rest. Rosie is going to be in recovery for a long time. We will need our strength. I'll stay a bit longer and let you know if there's any news.'

I kissed her. Dad followed suit and squeezed her shoulder as he went past.

'Good job I didn't take Eve's helmet out of the box.'

There it was again, the need to fix on some trivial detail, a way of clinging to a scrap of normality.

'I'll see you back home.'

Sunday, 11 August 2013

'Did you sleep?'

Mum shook her head. A chair scraped on the floor. There was a stumble as Dad escaped into the garden to stare across the hills.

'What about you?' Mum asked. 'You look exhausted.'

'I don't know. I lay awake for hours, but I think I dropped off sometime.'

Mum must have been up early. Rosie's bag was packed and sitting by the front door, ready to go. We met her at the hospital a couple of hours later. I will never forget the shattered look on her face.

'They took out the ventilator.'

'You mean she's on the mend?'

Her face crumpled. A choking groan followed.

'She's not right. She sat up mumbling. She was making these awful noises. It was so loud. You could hear it all over the ward. They had to sedate her.'

'But she was conscious,' I said. 'That's got to be an improvement.'

I was aware of Dad standing next to me. As Mum described Rosie's condition he let out a breath, but still said nothing.

'I don't know. I really don't know, but it doesn't feel

right. She wasn't . . . awake. It was a kind of reflex. Eve, I don't know what to make of it, but it scared me. This is worse than I thought.'

The day followed the same pattern as Saturday. Dad took me home while Mum stayed for a couple of hours. There was a call about seven o'clock.

'I've got to pick Mum up,' he said, reaching for his keys.

'But she's got the car.'

'She decided to drive over to see how Paul was doing. She lost control and smacked into some concrete bollards. I should have known she wasn't fit to drive.'

'Is she all right?'

'She's not hurt. She wasn't going fast. I don't think she's done any great damage to the car, either. She's in a terrible state. We'll be back soon.'

After twenty minutes I reached for the phone. I was going to call Jess, but I put it down without making the call. What could I say? I was in a dark place.

Monday, 12 August 2013

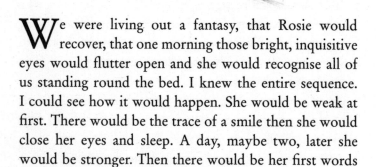

We were living out a fantasy, that Rosie would recover, that one morning those bright, inquisitive eyes would flutter open and she would recognise all of us standing round the bed. I knew the entire sequence. I could see how it would happen. She would be weak at first. There would be the trace of a smile then she would close her eyes and sleep. A day, maybe two, later she would be stronger. Then there would be her first words and the long, difficult journey back.

I got used to the hospital. It wasn't a second home. No institution that big, that clinical, could ever have the same warm familiarity as your own four walls, but I grew accustomed to its rhythms, the padding footsteps of the nurses, doctors, ancillary staff, their banter, jokes, smiles and occasional knowing looks. I absorbed its routines, the ambulances sliding into their bays, the visitors huddling round the vending machines, the boredom and frustration of the relatives. I got used to it, but, for all the help the staff gave us, hope crept ever closer to the exit. With every hour that passed it became more obvious that there wasn't going to be any good news about Rosie.

There were the questions the doctors asked. Did she

take drugs? Where was her partner, the boy who was hurt in the attack? It was as if nobody had explained to them what had happened. There didn't seem to be any coordination. They were groping towards an understanding of the events that had left Rosie broken and barely alive.

By then the police had assigned us a Family Liaison Officer. His name was George Howard. I don't know why, but his very presence shook me. If we had our own policeman, it had to be serious. The police were taking photographs, asking if the nurses could shave Rosie's hair so they could look for footprints. Mum was horrified by the requests. It was all part of Rosie's identity. Its loss seemed to demote her from a loved, cherished daughter and sister to some unrecognisable creature fit only for examination and analysis.

'Please don't,' she said, 'don't cut her hair.'

Mum sat by Rosie's side for hours on end, waxing her dreads, keeping them tidy. And that's how it was, Mum, Dad and I trying to cling on to our Rosie while all these machines and tests and photographs and questions took her away from us, transforming her into a case with a number. They took her off sedation and she made movements with her hands. Her legs twitched. The nurses got her sitting up, but her eyes were tracking, strange flickering, irregular movements that terrified me.

'Mum, why are her eyes doing that?'

That's when we knew for sure, when we saw her fitting. She was damaged. Our Rosie wasn't there. In place of my sister there was somebody half-alive, somebody who had to be fed by tubes, surrounded by stands and machinery. Horrible things were happening. Her stomach filled with water. Her tummy was rippling with it. Our tiny Rosie was bloating. From then on, the nightmare started to accelerate.

The doctor called us into a room. He was tall and shaven-headed. His scalp gleamed under the artificial light.

'What I have to say to you,' he began, 'will come as no surprise. Rosie is gravely ill.'

Finally there was the worst news of all.

She had had a heart attack.

Wednesday, 21 August 2013

That was the day Paul came to see her. He was on the slow path to recovery. The ordeal had gone on and on, the visits, the tests. Eleven days had passed since the night of the attack. By then we knew that Rosie wasn't coming back. At first they had talked about a partial recovery, maybe some speech and mobility problems. Then, with each day that passed, the predictions of improvement became lessened.

But Paul had returned. He was weak, and full fitness was a long way off, but he was the Paul we knew, the man who loved my sister. They brought him in a wheelchair and he stared at her with eyes dulled by suffering.

The police were putting together a kind of jigsaw. They had Paul's statement, but other things were happening. George had been telling Mum and Dad not to speak to the press. But there were others who didn't keep quiet, anonymous voices from the Brierley Hill estate.

People were messaging on the internet. We were in a bubble of grief and despair, but information about the killers kept washing up against our walls. We knew who was in the frame. It was the same names over and over again. Soon those names would have faces. When Paul had gone Mum took me out into the corridor.

'I've come to a decision.'

'About what?'

'About the boys who did this. I know how good George has been, but he can't tell me what to do. I can't keep quiet.'

'You're going to talk to the media?'

'I'll talk to anybody who is willing to listen. I will not be silent about what they did to my child. People have got to know.'

'What does Dad say?'

'He's finding it hard to handle what's happened. I've got to make a hard choice. It's going to affect your life, Eve. Are you OK with that?'

I could barely breathe. How do you answer a question like that? No, I wasn't OK with it. Maybe I was like Dad. I wanted it all to go away. I wanted the impossible. I wanted that story of recovery. Why couldn't there be a miracle? That's what it was like in the movies. If this had been a film, a nurse would have come racing down the corridor. Light would have flooded through the curtains and my sister would be there, with life in her eyes and a word of recognition on her lips. There would be swelling music. There would be a happy ending.

'Mum, you know best.' I fiddled with a tissue. 'What made you change your mind?'

'It was last night. It must have been two or three in the morning. A woman came up to me and put her arms round me. There she was, a complete stranger, but she had heard what those boys did to Rosie and she had something to say. Her husband is dying in another ward. Do you know what she said? She whispered in my ear, "You have to get this out. Tell people what they did to that girl of yours."

The moment she said it, I knew she was right. We will never have justice by keeping quiet and playing by the rules. If Rosie's life is going to mean something, we will have to fight for her.'

From that moment Mum began to fight and Dad and I slid into the background.

Friday, 23 August 2013

I had never seen anyone die before. I had never seen anyone really ill. Isn't it strange? The moment we accepted that Rosie was really gone, the moment we agreed that they could take the machines off, that was the first time she became human again. That was why Mum protected her hair the way she did. She wasn't going to let them strip her of everything she had been in life. In a way, no matter how painful those last few minutes were, that was when we had Rosie back.

We took it in turns to be with her and cuddle her, to say our goodbyes or let our farewell be a silent one, as it was with Dad. I had expected her to go suddenly, a flicker that was extinguished in a second. It wasn't like that. She continued breathing for twenty minutes on her own before she slipped away.

She had died long before, of course. We clung to our impossible dream, but she had been dead for two weeks. She was never going to survive. The doctors said she had two kinds of brain damage. That's what persuaded my parents to accept the inevitable. Mum was the last to hold her.

'The world is going to see this,' she said as we left the ward.

I didn't know what she had in mind. I couldn't have imagined all those meetings, the hours on the phone and the computer, the speeches and interviews. The only thing I knew was that Dad understood what it would mean and he couldn't go with her on her quest for justice. He would know that what Mum was doing was right, he would never stand in her way, but he would forever be in that room, watching those machines and tubes entangling his daughter. He had waded through horror and he refused to return to it. He would shut it out or it would destroy him. That's how my mum and dad started to drift apart. That's how they lost each other.

Monday, 11 November 2013

Did I say that we got Rosie back? In the days that followed it felt as if they did everything they could to tear her away from us again.

The battle began the moment she stopped breathing. They started to dictate how we would say goodbye. They wouldn't let us cremate her in case they had to dig her back up to get evidence. The whole thing became surreal. The police and the coroner said things that you couldn't dream up even in the most bizarre story. Rosie died on 23 August, but she would not be buried for three long months. There was no forensic expert available who dealt with brain injuries, so we had to wait. There was even talk that the burial might be as late as January. It was like the garbled retelling of a really sick movie. I was buried alive and I could hear the voices of the gravediggers above me.

One day George Howard visited the house. I was in the kitchen when I heard him say the most incredible thing.

'Dave, Cath, there is another option. You can bury her without her brain. When you get the brain back you can bury it with her body.'

We didn't know about autopsies and forensics and procedures, but we knew that this was yet another torture. So Mum went to the media. She did interviews. She wrote articles. She told them the situation. We couldn't bury our Rosie. In the end the authorities relented. There was a kind of victory. The funeral would be in November.

We weren't the only ones who stood up for Rosie. The goth community rallied round. They staged gigs and gatherings. Brierley United held a minute's silence for Rosie. The bandstand in Cartmel Park was transformed into a carpet of flowers, and the floral tributes were being refreshed on an almost daily basis. In a lonely moment, whenever there was another macabre twist to the long story of her journey from death to burial, I would wander down there and stand reading the tributes. The council voted in favour of setting up a plaque in her memory on the spot where the attack happened.

So the funeral, when it came, was both a celebration of Rosie and her life and a cry for justice. No one was religious so it was a humanist ceremony. My parents had always said that Heaven and Hell were here on Earth.

The hearse stopped down the road from Shackleton Crematorium where it was to be held. Hundreds of mourners had turned out to pay their respects, many of them in their gothic black. There were the alternative tribes Rosie had counted as friends: the Emos, the Punks, the Metallers, even Skaters. Mum and Dad had encouraged them to come dressed any way they wanted. Rosie was killed for the way she looked. On the day we let her go, nobody was going to pretend to be something they weren't.

Rosie had a white coffin. Family and friends escorted her along the road to the hall. Paul had recovered enough to accompany her. A lone piper played a lament and it danced on the snapping wind as we made our way in to the service. Every one of us carried a single rose.

The hall was decorated with Paul's portraits of Rosie. Her face was everywhere, studied or beaming, brooding or mischievous. I glimpsed Jess a few rows back and gave her a half-smile. Mum read the address:

'Rosie was a one-off. She was intelligent, enquiring and perceptive. She had her own mind, strong opinions and principles, but that is not why she died. She died because she dared to be different. She died because she expressed her individuality through the way she dressed, the way she made up her face and wore her hair. In a world that is becoming ever more uniform and homogenous, she made her life into a statement that was fiery and personal.

'That was her crime, to be herself. One August night a group of boys were drinking in a local park and they saw her as a threat. They looked at the dark clothes and the pale make-up and they saw somebody to mock and hurt and ultimately destroy. This is an appalling tragedy. It is a tragedy because ignorance can destroy beauty. Brutality can crush aspiration. Hatred can shatter hope.

'It is hard, so very hard, to come to terms with such cruel, mindless, brutish acts, but we must not give in to despair. We must never surrender to violence. Young or old, black or white, male or female, gay or straight, conventional or alternative, we all deserve the same respect. These values informed Rosie's life. That is why we remember her. Sleep tight, sweet child.'

There were other readings, mostly by Rosie's friends. I caught phrases, snatches of words, but no more than that. In my head we were scampering across the grass in our bare feet, Rosie seven or eight, me three or four, the summer sunlight on our faces. I ran behind, wanting to be like her. Now I would always be trailing in her wake, running after her rippling skirts forever as her spirit haunted the hills and cried for justice. I wept that morning, and it was partly for Rosie, but mostly for myself. Even then I was selfish. She had left a hole in the universe and I could never begin to fill it.

Paul went to her coffin, leaned forward and pressed his lips to the lid. It was the kiss of a man who has come back from the dead, but has left somebody he loved behind in the shadows. One by one at first, then in ever-growing groups, the mourners went forward and wrote their messages in felt-tip pen, black on the surface of the casket. Then it was a short walk to the plot where Rosie would lie beneath a yew tree, wind-ravaged and twisted by the storms that whipped off the moors. There were poems by Keats and Shelley, then a tall, lean man emerged from the crowd of mourners. He had a mane of raven-black hair.

'My name is Marcus Gould,' he said. 'I am the lead singer of Cast a White Shadow.'

This was one of Rosie's favourite bands. They were very bleak and lyrical.

'I am humbled that Rosie loved our music. I met her at the Whitby Goth Weekend one time. Rosie had to be different. She was wearing some kind of punk get-up, with a tartan skirt and torn leggings. She told me she would like to write a song for me to sing. That will never happen now, but I can read a poem for her to mark her passing. Nothing will hurt you now, Rosie. Be at peace.'

Then he closed his eyes and read the poem from memory, intoning it like some magical spell:

'You climbed to the top of the hill
And there you held the night by the hand
And the moon was high
And your future beyond the clouds
Was as bright as Sirius.

You did not know then
That there were people
Who lived in shadows,
And never saw
The brightness in the sky.
You stood at the top of the hill
And the night wind fluttered
In your hair, your skirts,
And no earthbound thing
Could hurt you.

You did not know then
That there were people
Whose eyes were closed
To the light of Sirius
And could not see beyond the clouds.

You climbed to the top of the hill
And the distant sea
Boomed and roared and shouted
To you to ride its mighty waves
And travel far beyond our shores.

You did not know then
That there were people

Who did not hear the waves
Or the singing of the sea
And were deaf to music.

You led me to the top of the hill
And you held me by the hand
And the moon was high,
But you left me then
To watch the light of Sirius alone.'

There was no applause. It wouldn't have been right. So we walked away, each with our own thoughts whispering in our minds. Jess caught up with me. I still remember what she said.

'I want to comfort you, Evie, but I don't know how. Why do words fail when you need them most? Oh God, if anything like that happened to my brother, I don't know what I would do.'

SO WHAT HAPPENS NOW?

Monday, 17 March 2014

They called it a cooling-off period. I was to stay off school for the rest of the week and for the trial. Anthony would also stay at home for a day or two. It would give things 'time to settle down' as Mr McKechnie put it. I wondered how the loss of my sister or the breakup of my parents' marriage would settle down. It wasn't like waiting for a headache to go. This was a pain so sharp, so real, sometimes I doubled up with it. Anthony had stood by while they kicked Rosie to death. Even after that, he had refused to act as a witness. In my eyes, there was no way back for him, no matter how he pleaded for forgiveness. He was beyond redemption.

The trial was in Preston, at the Crown Court. We parked in the multi-storey car park across the road and made our way over to the red brick building with its curved canopy entrance. It looked a bit like a school at first glance.

I had seen victims' families on the news before. I had watched them descend the steps outside the court and cluster round to make their statement to the press. Their faces were always grim. They always said the same thing. They were serving a life sentence. I was only now beginning to understand what they meant. I had had this idea that the trial would bring some kind of closure. Seeing how mean and ordinary the temple of justice really was, I no longer had any confidence that the verdict would solve anything. Whatever happened, the killers would live and Rosie would remain in her white casket in a Lancashire crematorium.

Mum went in to see the barrister. The seating area was a kind of long gallery in which the calm, the twitchy, the depressed and the arrogant gathered. I could see people from the other cases that were being heard the same day. There were family members who looked deeply ashamed to be there, but still others who took it in their stride, talking loudly about previous appearances, treating the whole process with contempt.

My phone buzzed and I glanced at the screen.

Thinking of you. Jess x.

Then Mum was back.

'Nothing much is going to happen today,' she said. 'They are all pleading guilty to Section 18.'

'What's that?'

'Grievous bodily harm with intent. Assault basically.'

'Is that it?' I cried. 'Assault? They killed her!'

Mum gave me a reassuring smile.

'I haven't finished, love. One of them is pleading guilty to murder.'

'Does that mean it's over?' I asked, more in hope than belief. 'What about Bradley Gorman?'

I heard the catch in her voice.

'He is pleading guilty to Section 18, but not guilty to murder.'

'You're joking!'

Mum could barely say the other boys' names.

'This one had blood on his socks and in his trainers. The evidence against him is overwhelming. There is less forensic evidence against Gorman. He thinks he can get away with GBH.'

'So what happens now?'

'The barrister has tomorrow to rewrite the prosecution. Bradley Gorman will face trial for murder alone on Wednesday.'

We sat through the proceedings. My gaze wandered over to the defendant closest. For a second he met my look. When he was charged with GBH, he caught my eye again and my heart thudded. I leaned over to Mum, revulsion choking off my breath.

'Do they even care?'

Tuesday, 18 March 2014

J ess was as true as steel from start to finish. She came round every evening to tell me what was happening in school. Mostly, she just sat while I talked, which was a change. It was usually the other way round.

'He smirked. But wasn't he ashamed?'

'None of them were. You should have seen the way they sat in court, lounging back in their seats, staring up at the ceiling while the clerk read out what they had done. Jess, it was unbelievable. Do you know we bumped into their families on the way out?'

'What happened?'

'Nothing really. Nobody said anything. It was the way they looked at us, as if we were the ones who had done something wrong.'

Jess grimaced.

'I'm glad I've never had to meet people like that.'

'But you have. What about Jake Lomas and Connor Hughes?'

'Eve, Jake and Connor are disgusting, but they're not like those killers, for goodness' sake. They're stupid little boys who can't grow up. Seriously, don't worry about Connor. He's more to be pitied than blamed.'

'I bet that's what Rosie thought when she saw those

guys waiting for her. These people don't go round with "psycho" tattooed on their foreheads. Something takes over, a kind of pack instinct.' I took her hands. 'They played a tape in court.'

'Tape?'

'It was a recording of a call to the emergency services. The onlookers weren't all like Anthony. One witness, a girl, phoned 999 for an ambulance. There was a recording of the message.'

'What did it say?'

'You could hear her crying over and over again, "We need an ambulance at Cartmel Park. These lads have banged a mosher for no reason. His girlfriend is on the ground too. Everyone is still on them, kicking them and stuff."' I struggled to carry on. 'Oh God, Jess, there were voices in the background shouting for them to get off.'

'Eve . . .'

'This poor girl who tried to help, she was pleading with the phone operator not to let anyone know who she was. She was terrified of what the gang might do to her. That's what it must be like knowing those animals.'

Jess's head sagged forward.

'And Anthony must have witnessed all that.'

Thursday, 20 March 2014

Rehana and Hannah waited up the road from the school gates.

'What's this,' I asked, 'moral support?'

Rehana linked arms.

'Something like that. Are you OK?'

'A bit nervous.'

'You've no need to be,' Jess said. 'You did what you had to. People admire you for it.'

'You drew attention to Anthony Broad and the scum who attacked your sister,' Hannah said. 'You're a legend.'

I didn't feel like a legend. My chest was crushed in a vice. All I could see was a figure in black spraying her bottle of fake blood then dissolving into tears. As heroic gestures went, it was pretty pathetic. I wasn't Eve Morrison, Year 11, mousey-haired, five foot four with a bum that bit too big and hips a bit too broad. I was the kid whose sister died, the kid who threw blood. I was the Fury. As we approached the pupil entrance with its electronically operated door, its worn, blue carpets, I wanted to run, to escape to the hills, just me, like a statue, gazing down at the world without thoughts, without memories, without pain and regret. I wanted to be the girl from Marcus Gould's poem. I wanted to accept the invitation to ride the mighty waves and travel far beyond England's shores, far beyond Shackleton and Brierley and the sordid proceedings at Preston Crown Court. I wanted to be a creature like Rosie, free of the crawling entrails of death, retribution and justice. Was that too much to ask, to be free, to be at peace with the world, to just be me?

AN ENDLESS VOID

Friday, 4 April 2014

I had one last day off school for the final day of the trial. The first defendant stood to hear the verdict. Even at that moment I thought I saw a smirk at the edges of his mouth. The judge's final remarks were brief.

'You have been found guilty of murder. You attacked without provocation, beating two innocent people to the ground and kicking one of them to death. You acted without conscience and you have shown no remorse. A date will be set for sentencing.'

His mother sat impassively while the judge ordered that the names of all five defendants be made public. I got up to leave the court and glimpsed a familiar face. Dad was two rows behind us.

'How long have you been there?' I asked.

'I slipped in half an hour ago.'

We stood in front of the court in bright sunlight while the press waited for the policeman in charge of the case to speak. George Howard was next to Mum while his boss, Detective Superintendent Anne Walker, made a statement. Dad declined an invitation to step forward.

'This is the most violent case I have had to deal with in my entire career,' DS Walker said. 'Even now I do not think that the brutality of this attack has been acknowledged.

The attackers assaulted two innocent young people. They revelled in kicking them and stamping on them while they lay helpless on the ground. Their victims were unable to defend themselves.'

Mum stepped forward. Her voice was firm and clear, but I noticed her fingers twitching away behind her back. Instinctively, I knew what she wanted and took her hand in mine. She was cold, so cold.

'On behalf of my family, I would like to thank the police for their efforts in bringing Rosie's attackers to court.'

I glanced back at Dad. Reluctantly, he shuffled forward. 'We are proud to have known Rosie. She was funny and gentle, caring and brave. In contrast to the five youths who set upon Paul and Rosie, she was full of empathy for others. She was a joy to know and love. We will never see her grow to be the confident, successful woman I know she would have become. She will never walk through the door and shout hello. I would give everything I own just to see her smile once more and call me Mum.'

That's where the horror really lay. How could she be gone? I linked Mum's arm and leaned into her. My head was on her shoulder.

'There is one more thing I have to say. This is not an isolated incident. I hope that people seeing this on their television sets will realise that we are all different in our own ways. That is what makes us human. I hope that they will spread the word that nobody deserves to be attacked for the way they choose to dress. Thank you.'

With that, it was over. Dad nodded briefly and slipped away outside the court. Mum and I walked to the car in silence. We stood in the echoing vastness of the car park, the slam of a door reverberating a few metres away.

'That's it then,' Mum said. 'Ready to go, love?'

'Give me a minute, eh?'

I walked to the wall of the car park and gazed down at the street below. People were hurrying this way and that, all on their way somewhere or on their way back. I felt so alone. Six months earlier I had known exactly what the future had in store for me, GCSEs, A levels, university. Life was OK. I knew where I was going. Suddenly all I could see ahead of me was an endless void.

Charlie found Anthony sitting alone on a bench at the back of the Science block. He had his blazer wrapped round him.

'You not going in for lunch?'

Anthony shook his head and handed him his phone.

'Have you forgotten what day it is?'

Charlie read the headline.

'Nothing you could have done, mate.'

'Yes, there was. Gollum tried to pull the attackers off. Then there was that girl. She called 999. I did nothing.'

'You were scared. It could happen to anyone.'

'It happened to me.' He pounded his fist on the bench. 'To me!'

Charlie handed the phone back.

'I don't even know what happened,' Anthony continued. 'Was I scared? It didn't feel like fear. It's as if I was standing behind one of those glass walls. I could see what was happening, but it didn't seem to be happening in the same world.' He shoved the phone in his blazer pocket. 'Do you understand that?'

Charlie raised his hand in a gesture that distanced himself.

'Anthony, how am I meant to understand what went on that night? It's not the kind of thing that happens very often, is it? I've only seen a couple of incidents of violence in my whole life, nothing heavy, a bit of push and shove, a few threats. That's it. All this . . .' He shook his head. 'It's way out of my experience.'

'I wish it had been way out of mine.' Anthony shuffled

to the left to let Charlie sit down.

'The way I see it, Anthony, you were in the wrong place at the wrong time. I don't know if there's anything you could have done. Only you know that. I can say this – you didn't kill that girl. You didn't egg them on. Mate, worst thing you did was to walk on by. So you're no Good Samaritan. Why do you think that story's such a big deal? It's not because people go to help. It's because they don't. The Good Samaritan is unusual, that's the point. People look the other way. That Gollum guy, he's some kind of hero for what he did.'

'Why can't we all be like him? I should have helped him. He begged me to.'

'You didn't, though, did you? There's nothing you can do to change it. You're going to have to find a way to live with it.'

'That's it, though, Charlie. I can't.'

My phone buzzed and danced on the window seat. I wasn't in any mood to talk, but I picked up anyway and read the caller ID.

'Hi Jess.'

'I saw you on TV. Was that your dad at the back?'

'Yes.'

'Your mum was fab, so strong.'

'She was, wasn't she?' Not me, though. 'Look, Jess, I'm not being funny, but let's talk about something else.'

'That's why I called. You need to get out of the house. Did you remember about the Bridleway Walk?'

The Bridleway was a six-hour loop around the valley. They had been holding the walk for three years now to raise money for charity. Shackleton had a link with some trust that helped get books and other materials into schools in Malawi.

'There's been too much going on. When is it?'

'Tomorrow.'

Of course, all those posters around school.

'Jess, I can't. Mum needs me.'

'Needs you for what?' she called.

I didn't know she was in the next room. I knew I was done for.

'It's the Bridleway Walk.'

'You should go. Get out of the house. It will do you good.'

I couldn't hide the sigh.

'OK, Jess,' I said. 'I'll be there. What time?'

'My dad's driving me to the starting point. We'll pick

you up at eight. You need a packed lunch, strong shoes, a waterproof coat.'

Another release of breath. 'I'll be ready.'

I hung up and found Mum in her room.

'What are you doing?'

'I found these old photo albums. Remember this?'

There were a few pages of snaps from our holiday in Florida. I must have been about seven. Rosie was eleven.

'I was already catching up with her then.'

'Yes, Rosie got really crabby about it.'

'Did she?'

'Not half. She was the big sister and she knew you would be towering over her within a couple of years.'

We turned the pages, laughing at the shared memories.

'All the love you put into your children. You change their nappies, wipe their noses, bath them, teach them their numbers and alphabet. You push them round in the pram, take them on days out, listen when they're upset, nurse them when they're ill. You do all that and somebody can destroy them in a second.'

'Oh, Mum, don't.'

'That policeman, he said we'd got justice. What does that mean? Those boys will go to prison, hopefully for a very long time, but they'll be alive. They will watch TV, play their computer games, have access to a gym. Their parents can visit them, hold them. I will never hold Rosie ever again.'

And I couldn't help myself. I had to say it.

'Mum, I'm still here. You can hold me.'

So she did. We sat together for a long time that evening, until the sun dimmed and it was time to cook the tea.

Saturday, 5 April 2014

'I feel a bit of a fraud,' I confessed as Jess's dad pulled away. 'I didn't get any of those sponsor sheets filled in. I'm not walking for charity. I'm . . . just walking.'

Oli put his arm round my shoulder.

'Eve, just walking is good. I think people understand you've had other things on your mind.'

'Has everybody been talking about the verdict at school?'

'What do you think?' he said. 'Don't worry about it. Everybody's on your side.'

'Really? Everybody?'

'Yes, the usual suspects apart. You're among friends here. Nobody's going to say anything you don't want to hear. Nobody's going to hurt your feelings.'

Jess gave me a hug.

'Oli's right. Enjoy the day.'

There was quite a crowd. They were squatting on rocks, lounging on the grass, tying laces, swigging from water bottles. They were wearing a collection of boots, trainers, jeans, leggings and cagoules. There were bobble hats of every description, from the football-branded to the Norwegian ones with the tassles. Some of the walkers were flapping at the flies that were weaving lazy patterns in the air. Rehana and Hannah jogged over the moment they saw us.

'Hi guys. When do we set off?'

'Ask Mrs Rawmarsh. She's the boss.'

So I did. She was lacing her boots. She looked different away from school, younger, more like us really.

'Mrs Rawmarsh, when do we start?'

'Any minute,' she said, as Ian Wilkinson scrambled out of his mum's car. 'Here's our final walker. Hurry up, Wilko, we're ready to roll.'

I turned to relay the news to the others. Simultaneously, Mrs Rawmarsh caught my arm. She wanted a word before we set off. This was getting repetitive. Suddenly I was the girl with a thousand agony aunts.

'Oh, Eve.'

'Yes?'

'We're not in school. I'm here on behalf of the trust, so today it's Joanna.' She gave a half-smile. 'Are you OK?'

'I'm fine.'

We climbed the steep gradient to the first summit. There was a sweeping view of the cobalt-blue reservoirs and the emerald hills. Instinctively I found myself gazing into the distance, half expecting to see Rosie standing there. She was gone, of course, but she would always be there, as somebody I loved and as somebody to whom I would always be compared. She would be there because I wasn't her and I never would be. She was there because she was no longer a sister or a daughter, but an icon, the murdered innocent.

Images stuttered through my mind, of those endless hours in the hospital, of the night of the talent contest, of the trial and the verdict. It was all in the past, but where was the future?

We trekked for two and a half hours through the wild, rugged country. I didn't think it was possible to leave death and retribution behind, but I surrendered to its beauty and discovered a kind of unexpected quiet. I found myself next to Oli.

'You're being really brave, Eve,' he said.

'Me?'

'What you did the night of the talent competition.'

'You think that was brave? Everybody else thinks I went crazy.'

'No, they don't. It takes guts to take a stand.'

'Like you did.'

He smiled.

'Suddenly everybody's making a statement.' He punched the air playfully. 'Go us.'

Reaching the top of the rise, I nudged him in the ribs.

'Race you.'

I started to hurtle down the steep path on the other side, yelling for all I was worth, screaming out all the anxiety and tension that had been building and building for months. I was almost out of control. Any moment I would pitch forward and crash down onto the sharp, uneven stones. I didn't care. Damn the stones. Damn pain and blood and death. Oli caught up and grabbed my arm.

'You watch you don't break your neck,' he panted.

I turned.

'You take care of yourself too, Oli.'

He frowned.

'Meaning?'

'Connor. His father is . . .'

'A thug. I know. Jess told me.'

'Just be careful, yeah?'

'You got it.'

At that moment Jess appeared, wriggled between us and linked our arms.

'Hey, my two favourite people.'

The sun came out and fell on our faces and far in the distance, barely there at all, was an inky storm cloud.

BURIED ALIVE

Wednesday, 9 April 2014

Anthony leaned forward, head resting against the wall, palms splayed like insects.

'Do I really have to go?'

'Yes, you have to. We both have to. We are going to walk in there with our heads held high. We are going to parents' evening because we can't let this dominate the rest of our lives. I will not allow that to happen. I know what it's like to be scared, Anthony.'

She dug her nails into his arm.

'Don't look away. You're going to hear this. I understand fear. That's what you felt that night, fear. You were paralysed by it.'

'Maybe. That's not how it felt.'

'That's how it *was*. Anthony, you are a sensitive, intelligent lad. You're not like those animals. Life has to begin again. We don't deserve this. It's as if we are buried alive in the coffin along with Rosie Morrison. Please come with me tonight.'

It took him some time to recover himself. Finally, he nodded.

'OK, I'll go.'

I felt Mum stiffen.

'What is it?'

'Anthony Broad and that mother of his.' She squeezed my arm. 'Let's try to forget about them. This evening is about my brave, intelligent daughter. Who's first?'

'Mrs Desai. English is my best subject.'

Oli came over wearing the biggest smile I had ever seen. He was enjoying his role as an ambassador for the school. It made him skittish. He acted very gallantly, making a sweep with his right arm.

'This way, ladies. May I say how lovely you both look this evening?'

I laughed. 'Oli, stop it.'

'Hey, stop fighting with my brother,' Jess called, hurrying across. 'That's my job.' She took my arm. 'Who've you seen so far?'

'Nobody. We're on our way to Mrs Desai. What about you?'

'Mr Jackson says I only exercise one part of my body in PE lessons and that's my mouth! What do you think of that?'

'Pretty accurate, really.'

She pretended to swat me.

'I'll leave you to your glowing report from Mrs Desai.'

She had Mum's attention.

'So I'm going to hear nice things?'

'Are you kidding? Mrs Desai thinks the sun shines out of Eve.'

'She does not!'

'You get the best marks in the whole year.'

Mum stared.

'You never told me that. I knew you were bright, but
. . . Why do I have to hear this second hand?'

I shrugged and steered her towards Mrs Desai.

'You've got a good friend there,' Mum said. 'I've always
liked Jess. And Oli is such a lovely lad.'

'I know,' I said. 'They're the best.'

Anthony and his mother were almost out of the door when Mrs Rawmarsh caught up with them.

'Mrs Broad? Do you mind if we have a brief word?'

Anthony saw his mother look around the rapidly emptying hall. Oli Hampshire and Freya Morton were starting to stack the chairs and tidy up. He noticed Jess waving goodbye to her brother as she left with her parents. He ached to make things right with her, but he knew that was impossible. He found himself eavesdropping on the conversation.

'I wish you were coming back with us in the car,' Mrs Hampshire was saying.

'Don't worry, Mum. I'm fine on my scooter.'

'Just be careful. Drivers don't always consider motorcyclists.'

Some of the teachers were packing away ready to go. Mrs Rawmarsh was still trying to persuade Anthony's mother to spare her five minutes.

'I don't want to miss our bus. They're every half hour at this time.'

'Just a couple of minutes, Mrs Broad. Please.'

'Is Anthony in some kind of trouble?'

'No, nothing like that. I thought I'd touch base, see how you were both getting on.' She checked that nobody was listening. 'That scene at the talent show must have been quite distressing for you.' She gave the almost deserted hall another glance. 'Listen, I waited until the very end. I just wanted to know you were both OK.'

'We'll get through it.'

'Is that how you feel too, Anthony? Things *will* get better. I promise.'

Anthony shrugged. By the time they stepped outside, the last cars were queuing to turn on to the main road. Headlights swept the darkness as they pulled out of the school grounds.

'That was nice of her.'

Anthony noticed Connor Hughes over by the bike sheds. He didn't remember seeing him at parents' evening.

'Anthony, are you listening to me? I said, that was nice of Mrs Rawmarsh.'

'Yes, she's all right.'

Connor saw him looking and turned away. Anthony frowned.

'Come on, we'll have to hurry to get that bus.'

They started to jog. That's when he noticed the white van parked across the road from the main gates. The driver was looking towards the school. A tattooed arm rested in the open window. There was another man in the passenger seat. The way they kept glancing back into the van suggested that there was at least one more person with them.

'Anthony! It's coming.'

He didn't move. Who were they waiting for? There were very few people left inside. Anthony's gaze drifted across the car park. Freya Morton was getting into her mum's car. Suddenly she stopped. She was talking to somebody. Oli came into view.

'Anthony, where are you going? Come on. The bus is here.'

He took no notice. He was more interested in Oli and

Freya and the watcher in the van. He caught a snatch of their conversation.

'Oh, Oli, who would do that? I would offer you a lift, but we're going the opposite way. We're calling on my nan.'

'Don't worry about it, Freya. I'll get the bus. Maybe I'll walk. It's not that far.'

'And you say somebody slashed both tyres?'

Oli nodded.

'Yes, my scooter's going nowhere. It was intentional, all right. I'll have to leave it overnight and get it sorted in the morning.'

'Honestly, some people. That's just mindless vandalism. I'll see you in the morning.'

'Yes, goodnight.'

The car pulled away and took a left onto the main road. That's when Anthony saw Connor. None of this was a coincidence. It was happening again. He was standing behind the same veil, waiting for the horror to unfold. Connor was getting out of the back of the van. The driver and the man in the passenger seat joined him. One had a baseball bat, the other a wheel wrench. It was at that moment Anthony knew his instincts were right. This time he smashed through the glass wall.

'Mum, find somebody quick. Phone the police. They're going to get Oli.'

'Anthony, what are you talking about? Where are you going?'

Oli was out of the school gates and walking along the opposite pavement. He was oblivious to the approaching figures. Anthony heard his mother call his name, but he ignored her. Connor and the two men were running toward Oli. He still hadn't seen them. Anthony found his voice.

'Oli, run!'

Oli heard the shout and turned. He looked up and saw the attackers. There was only one way to go, left into the side road. Anthony could still hear his mother screaming somewhere behind him, but he wasn't going to stop. Charlie had been right. There was a way back and this was it.

'Where is he, Brian? Did you see which way he went?'
Brian Hughes glared at his brother.

'Stop shouting my name all over the street. Do you want to see me back inside?' He noticed Connor. 'Get back in the bloody van. I don't want anybody seeing you.'

'Dad, are you sure about this?'

His father's stare made him flinch.

'You listen to me, boy. No loud-mouthed poof makes a fool of my son.'

Connor slunk over to the vehicle.

'Right, let's get this over with.'

Colin Hughes strained to see.

'I can't make out a thing. He's gone to ground.'

'He can't have gone far. You stay here where you can keep an eye on the whole street. I'm going to check the alleys.'

'What if he's got away?'

'He hasn't. We didn't hear any footsteps. Take my word for it, the queer's here somewhere.'

He started pulling wheelie bins away from walls and poking behind them with the baseball bat.

'Where are you, you poof? You were keen enough to come out, or whatever you call it. Yes, quick enough to take the piss out of my boy in front of everybody, and all. You're not so ready to face me, are you?'

He moved on to the next alley. Suddenly, a dark figure propelled the wheelie bin into him and started to run.

'There he goes!'

Brian and Colin Hughes had their man.

Anthony's blood ran cold. Oli was younger and fitter than his pursuers. He was beginning to leave them toiling in his wake. That's when the white van screamed across the top of the road. Its tyres squealed as it braked hard, blocking his way. He had been right. Connor wasn't the only one in the back. There had been another man and he was now at the wheel. He was in his late teens or early twenties, an older brother Anthony guessed. He opened the door and grinned.

Oli hesitated. They were on him in a second. The bat swung, catching Oli a glancing blow on the temple that knocked him half-senseless. His chest and face struck the pavement, a low grunt bursting from him. There was blood on his lips. Anthony saw the glint of the wheel brace and threw himself at Colin's arm. Colin flung Anthony aside with ease.

'So who the hell are you, his boyfriend?'

Anthony could only pant the simplest answer. He said the words he had failed to find in Cartmel Park.

'Let him be.'

'Who asked you to interfere?' Brian Hughes yelled. 'Do you want some too? Well, do you?'

The uproar had brought people to their windows. The Hughes brothers saw the living room lights through the open curtains and blinds and the silhouetted figures peering out. This wasn't going as planned.

'Leave it, Brian, they've both got the message. There's no point getting ourselves arrested over this.'

Brian Hughes pointed the baseball bat at Anthony's head.

'I'll remember your face, you interfering little scumbag. Now clear off while you can still walk.'

Anthony could only stare at him dumbly. There was no glass wall. This was fear, pure and simple.

Hughes jabbed Anthony's shoulder, making him stumble backwards. The brothers laughed. Brian Hughes turned and drove his boot into Oli's ribs.

'Watch your back, you shirtlifting scum. You never know who's going to be behind you.' Then he turned, very deliberately and very slowly, and saw Anthony. 'I thought I told you to go.'

Without any further warning, he swung the bat.

Thursday, 10 April 2014

A nthony sat up when the door went.
'You came.'

Oli perched on the edge of the bed.

'What did you expect? Anything could have happened in that street. They could have killed me. What you did . . . I owe you, mate.'

Anthony's gaze shifted to the third person in the room.

'I don't know what to say,' Jess told him.

'So don't say anything. I just hope . . . I don't want you to feel that I betrayed you. If you can wipe the slate clean, that's enough. It's all I've ever wanted.'

Jess nodded. Satisfied, Anthony turned back to Oli. 'How are you?'

Oli touched his forehead. 'They gave me this bruise to remember them by.'

'Looks nasty.'

'I've got a few scratches too, but you can see those. There's no real damage. It will be gone in a few days. My ribs are sore. Other than that, I'm fine. A bit shaken, that's all. I was too cocky by half. I knew Connor bore a grudge, but I didn't expect anything like this.' He waited a beat. 'So what about you?'

'They kept me in overnight for observation. They did a

brain scan. It's all clear. I can go home later. Mum's gone back to the flat to get a change of clothes.'

'My dad's outside in the corridor,' Jess said. 'We could run you home.'

Anthony held her gaze. 'No, we'll get a taxi. Thanks anyway. Do you know what's going to happen to the men who attacked you? What about Connor?'

'The word is, Connor is going to be permanently excluded. I don't know how true it is. Some of the neighbours got photos of the van's number plate.'

'The police have interviewed Brian and Colin Hughes and Connor's older brother Gary. There hasn't been any more news.'

When the conversation ran thin, Anthony posed the question he had been keeping in reserve, the one he had been aching to ask.

'Has Eve said anything?'

'No, but you might be able to ask her yourself.'

'She's here?'

'I wanted her to come in with us. She refused.'

'I'd like to see her.'

Jess walked to the door.

'I'll ask.'

They left us alone to talk. It was strange seeing him there on the bed. His skin was ashen, his hair untidy. He looked more like a little boy than a teenager. I spoke first.

'You finally did something.'

'Better late than never.'

I let a raised eyebrow pass verdict on that comment.

'Why?' I asked. 'Why last night?'

'I don't understand.'

I made it simple for him.

'Why were you able to stand up for Oli when you couldn't stand up for Rosie? What made you act for him and not for her?'

'It's complicated.'

'I've got plenty of time.'

'Will you hear me out?'

I nodded.

'What happened in Cartmel Park, it's like some crazy nightmare. Do you understand what I'm saying?'

'I'm listening.'

He was struggling to make sense of my answer. Well, tough, I didn't want to be there. Jess was the only reason I was even in the room. If this had to happen it was going to be on my terms, not his. He didn't deserve any more than that.

'I'd been living in fear for months. I was a basket case. Mosley had made me scared of my own shadow. That night . . .'

He rubbed away the tears that had started to come with a pyjama sleeve that was too long for his arm.

'That night, when they attacked Rosie . . . Eve, for once it wasn't me being hit. It wasn't me being pushed around. It's horrible . . . I hate myself . . . The reason I didn't say anything is because, as long as they were picking on Paul and Rosie, no one was picking . . .' He pounded his chest with his fist. 'No one was picking on me.'

His eyes pleaded with me for a response. I stared him down.

'I didn't think she was going to die. Things like that don't happen in real life, only in movies. People don't get murdered for nothing, not here, not in a little place like

Brierley. I thought . . . I thought she would have some bruises, that's all.'

'Liar!'

'What?'

'You're a liar, Anthony.' I didn't want to hurt him. I wanted him to face the truth. 'You could see what was happening. They kicked her in the head. They stamped on her again and again and again.' I brought down my fist in time with the words. 'You don't come away from violence like that with *bruises*. Oh, you were glad it wasn't you lying there on the floor, but don't lie to yourself. You didn't care what they did, so long as nothing happened to *you*. That's it, isn't it? You thought if you tried to protect her, you were going to get hurt. It was all about you.'

And that's when he broke down.

'Yes.'

My neck prickled.

'What?'

'Yes, Mosley turned me into a coward. I just didn't want to get involved.'

His chin dropped onto his chest. I stared down at him for thirty seconds, a minute, maybe longer.

'But you found it within you to save Oli?'

'Yes.'

'So you could have saved Rosie?'

His chest was heaving.

'I suppose so.'

'Could you have saved her?'

There was a pause of several seconds.

'Yes.'

Without another word, I started to walk to the door.

'Eve . . .'

'I thought we were done talking.'

'Eve please, I have to ask. I can't live with myself. Is there any way you can forgive me?'

I half-turned.

'You did something good when you fought to save Oli. Jess will do the forgiving.'

'But what about you? You're the one that matters. Can you forgive me?'

I completed the turn.

'I'm not a priest, Anthony. I can't give you absolution. Who am I to forgive anybody? I'm just as weak, just as ordinary, just as cowardly as you are. It's not me you have to ask for forgiveness.'

'So who do I ask? Eve, I can't live with this pain.'

'That's what we all want, you, me, my mum and dad, but it isn't possible. When they killed Rosie, they tore something out of all of us. You don't get over it. They say it heals. I don't believe that's true. It's been six months and I still can't close my eyes without seeing them swarming over her, stamping on her. It doesn't get better. It doesn't heal. Time doesn't make it go away. All you can do is find a way to carry on.'

'But who do I ask for forgiveness?'

'It's you, Anthony. You have to do it. So tell me, can you? Can you look yourself in the mirror and forgive yourself?'

He continued to stare before finally hanging his head. 'No.'

I continued to the door.

'That's your burden. I've spent six months trying to find a way to live with myself, Anthony. I think I'm about there now. Maybe one day you will find a way to forgive yourself. I wish you good luck.' I opened the door. For some reason I started to laugh. 'Do you know, I actually mean that. I want you to find a way back, but there's nothing I can do to help. I'm not that good a person.'

When I closed the door behind me, Jess reached for my hand. Her eyes were bright with expectation.

'Well, what happened?'

'We talked.'

'And?'

'And nothing. Life goes on. We carry on the way we were. I'll see you tomorrow, Jess.'

'That's it?'

'That's it.'

'But what happened?'

'If you're looking for a happy ending, Jess, there isn't one. We're not little kids any more. It's not the way things work.'

'I thought at least . . .'

I patted her arm.

'I know.'

She didn't press me any further.

'Do you want to come round to mine?'

'Not tonight. I'll see you tomorrow.'

I kissed her on the cheek. She was still trying to make sense of what I had told her. Things hadn't turned out the way she imagined. I walked out of the automatic doors. Dusk was gathering over the hills. I ran my gaze along the brow and satisfied myself that, for the first time in months, there was nobody there.

READER'S NOTES

IN BRIEF

On 10 August 2013, Eve waved goodbye to her big sister Rosie and Rosie's boyfriend Paul as they hopped on a bus. Six months later Eve's life is dramatically different. Her big sister – a lively, passionate girl who dressed in goth clothes, wore her hair in dreadlocks, loved her family and had many issues she strongly believed in – was attacked in Brierley on her way from a party. She died in hospital.

Six months later, Eve is back at school. Her parents have separated, her mum spends much of her time campaigning for justice for Rosie, and her best friend Jess is trying to be a good friend and sometimes getting it wrong. On a normal February day, Anthony arrives at Eve's school. She recognises him as someone connected with her sister's death. He was in the park the night Rosie died.

Eve's best friend, Jess, immediately develops a crush on Anthony, but is puzzled that Eve doesn't seem to like this new, mysterious boy in their class. At home, Jess's older brother Oli has decided to tell his parents that he is gay. Jess and her brother are close, and she promises to support him.

Anthony is finding settling into his new school

difficult. He and his mum are living in fear of her violent and abusive ex-boyfriend. Anthony is tormented by memories of the night Rosie died, and the fact that he stood by as the attack took place. Eve is persuaded by her mum not to cause any kind of scene at school because she wants Anthony to give evidence at the upcoming trial.

Meanwhile, Anthony makes a friend, Charlie, with whom he shares a love of music. Charlie persuades Anthony to audition for the school talent contest. It is a busy term, with the school debate final also coming up. Oli is one of the finalist speakers, and the topic for debate is 'Has political correctness gone too far?' As part of the debate, Oli refers to his own sexuality, coming out to the whole school. Two bullies, Jake and Connor, react, picking on Jess. Emotions are running high, and Jess and Eve clash about why Eve is so cold towards Anthony. Jess finds out about his connection to Rosie's death and promises to stand by her friend.

In the semi-final of the debate, Oli is the target of some mean and potentially embarrassing questions. He answers them well and, in the process, humiliates Jake and Connor. Eve is worried by this; her mum has warned her that Connor is part of the Hughes family, who have a reputation for violence.

Following Jess's support of Oli, Eve feels as though she has let Rosie down by not even trying to put pressure on Anthony to give evidence at the trial. Her mum has been equally unsuccessful. With the final of the school talent show approaching, which Anthony stands a good chance of winning, Eve plans a way to take revenge.

At the trial of the gang accused of murdering Rosie, Anthony does not give evidence. Eve realises that the trial, on which she and her mum had rested so many hopes and invested so much energy, will never be able to give her an outcome that makes her feel better.

Following the trial, Eve and Anthony are back at school. There is a Year 11 parents' evening and Jess, Eve and Anthony attend with their parents. Oli, as a sixth-form prefect, is helping out. At the end of the evening, Jess leaves with her parents, but Oli helps tidy up and has his scooter to get home on. Anthony and his mum are among the last to leave, and as they do, Anthony notices some men in a van watching Oli closely. He realises that the men are the Hughes family, and that Oli isn't going to get away. Neither of them can.

Anthony wakes up in hospital with Oli and Jess there to thank him for trying to protect Oli. Anthony asks to see Eve and tries to explain his actions, or rather his lack of action, on the night Rosie died. He asks if she can forgive him. Eve says that her forgiveness isn't the important thing; Anthony needs to be able to live with himself and forgive himself. She leaves the hospital feeling more at peace with the future.

FOR REFLECTION

Hate is an imagined story but the attack on Rosie and Paul has been drawn from a real-life attack. Sadly, hate crime is not as rare as we might imagine, in the UK and around the world.

When we read a novel like this, knowing how to process what we have read and how to think and respond to events like the ones in the story can be difficult. The following questions can be discussed with a friend or a book group, or could just be some ideas for you to think about.

- If you had to describe your identity and who you are in ten words, what would they be?

- Music is an important part of life for several of the characters in *Hate*. How important is music to you, your friends, and people you know? What things that are a part of popular culture can unite and divide people?

- How many groups can you think of that you belong to? Why do we join groups? Are humans drawn to feeling as if they need to belong to some kind of group?

What 'groups' can you see in the novel, and why did the characters 'join' them?

- Family is important to all the characters in *Hate*, although the families themselves are very different. Do you think, overall, that *Hate* suggests that families are always positive groups to belong to?

- Which characters do you see as having things in common? In particular, which characters do you think have things in common with Anthony? In the story, Eve finds comfort in being in the great outdoors. Is there a place where you find it easier to think, reflect and to be honest with other people? Why is this?

- Do you think the reaction that Oli's family had when he told them he was gay was a fair one? What reaction would someone receive in the groups you belong to if they told others that they were gay?

- 'You think the battle against prejudice is won? We get lessons and assemblies on equal opportunities. Everyone pretends to be all PC. Are you telling me you've never heard a racist or sexist joke? You've never heard the boys comparing the girls' boobs?' Are these comparisons that Eve makes (racist jokes and comments about girls' bodies) fair things to compare with homophobia and the sort of hate crime committed against Rosie and Paul?

- 'Every word had drawn blood'. Do you think words or physical actions are more damaging? Which characters in *Hate* do you think would agree and disagree with you, and why would they agree or disagree?

• Who in the story can be seen as a 'victim'? How would you define what we mean by a 'victim'?

• 'It takes a hell of a lot of people to do good. It only takes one or two to do evil.' Do you agree with what Eve's dad says here? Can you think of anyone who has done a lot of good by themselves?

• Lots of characters carry feelings of guilt in the book. Which characters feel guilty, and why? How do you think people can deal with feeling guilty after they have behaved in a way that they later regret?

• How did you feel towards Eve and towards Anthony at the beginning and end of the book? If you could ask each of them one question at the close of their stories, what would it be and why?

Following the murder of Sophie Lancaster,
her family wanted to create a lasting legacy to
their daughter and so The Sophie Lancaster
Foundation was established and became a
registered charity in 2009. To find out more visit
www.sophielancasterfoundation.com

Stonewall's Education for All campaign works
to tackle homophobic bullying and help schools
support lesbian, gay and bisexual young people.
Their website contains a range of resources
including research, teacher training guides,
lesson ideas and interactive DVDs for pupils.
www.stonewall.org.uk/atschool. The Young
Stonewall website also contains specific advice
and support for gay young people who might
be experiencing homophobic bullying or having
difficulties with issues such as coming out
www.youngstonewall.org.uk